Murder by the Letter

Carmen Radtke

Contents

Chapter 1

Frances Sullivan shivered. The London sky that only this morning had been streaked with hopeful blue, had turned leaden as soon as she and their newest family member had reached the green. Now, hail pelted her without mercy while she scooped up the puppy, cradled him to her chest, and ran for cover under a tall oak.

Above her head, a squirrel cowered under the dense foliage. Under normal circumstance, she'd put a peanut on the ground to watch the animal pick it up, but in this dismal weather, she only cared about her own and Leo's well-being. The little corgi snuggled deep into her arms.

She peered at the sky. Surely the hail must stop any moment, so she could dash home and dry herself and the puppy off.

Her teeth chattered. They had proper winters in Adelaide too, but not with this smoke-filled clogged air and the lack of sunshine. As much as she loved London, she couldn't wait to be back home in Australia, with its sunshine, the beach, and all their friends.

One more month and they'd sail back home, hopefully this time without another murder.

"Darling?" She spun around at the sound of a well-loved voice. There, with a large umbrella over his head, stood her husband. Despite her physical discomfort, a little glow spread inside her. She'd left

Adelaide in October 1931 as Frances Palmer, and here she stood four months later, as Mrs Jack Sullivan.

He held the umbrella, so it afforded her full protection. Leo gave a happy yip at the sight of his master, and Frances handed him over.

"I'm sorry I didn't catch up with you sooner," Jack said. "But we'll have you home and warm again in a twinkle."

She slipped her arm through his as he led her the shortest way to his mother's house where they were staying until their return home.

"It is beastly weather," she said. "I hope Uncle Sal stays out if it." Although Salvatore "the Magnificent" Bernardo was only her godfather and not her real uncle, she loved him almost as much as she adored Jack.

The only worry was Uncle Sal's health. Although he always insisted he was fit as a fiddle, his gammy ankle used to hurt and stiffen in the damp. The damage was the result of a car accident that had ended his stage career for good.

Well, almost ended. Since Jack and his night club in Adelaide had entered their lives, there had been a few occasions for the entertainer to take the spotlight again, with her as his assistant "Signorina Francesca" at his side. Better still, thanks to their combined acting skills, the three of them had solved several murders too.

"If the hail doesn't stop, I'll make sure he's safe from the elements," Jack promised. "That's what taxis are there for."

He held her back as they reached a busy road. Cars and a double-decker bus raced past, with their squealing tires splashing through the ankle-deep puddles. If Frances had stood closer to the kerb she'd have been drenched even worse.

"You poor darling," her mother-in-law, Katherine Parr, said as Jack bundled Frances through the door. "There's a hot bath waiting for you, and then I prescribe a sip of brandy to stave off a cold."

"Heavenly." Frances allowed herself to be taken upstairs.

The bathroom was filled with steam, and the delicious scent of Katherine's lavender bath salts made Frances sigh in bliss. She'd miss Jack's mum and her husband. They'd arranged the small wedding ceremony, and it was thanks to them that their guests had embarked on this adventure at all. Without Katherine's urgent wish to see her son, Frances would be sitting in Adelaide in the telephone exchange where she worked as an operator, and Uncle Sal would be doing his best to be useful around the house which he shared with Frances, her mother, and a lodger.

Instead, they'd made friends in the London society, been invited to the French Riviera for a New Year's Eve party, and she and Jack had had a spiffing honeymoon in Paris, as a reward for their assistance with a murder case.

She sank into the warm water and thought back to that magical week. Seven days, without other people to consider or duties to take care of – and with Jack. They'd strolled hand in hand along the Seine, dined in intimate restaurants, and then, at night ...

A whine outside the bathroom door interrupted her memories. Leo, a ten-week-old puppy named after da Vinci, had been another wedding present.

If she was honest, she appreciated his presence not only because he was irresistible, but also because walking him and caring for him gave her something to do. To be even more honest, the freedom of obligations which she'd looked forward to for so long had begun to lose its appeal.

She wondered if Jack felt the same. Back home, he ran the "Top Note", Adelaide's and maybe Australia's best night club. He took care of his staff who consisted mostly of soldiers who'd served under Captain Jack Sullivan, and he made sure his people would be fine, no matter how bad times were in the Great Depression that filled the streets everywhere with hungry and unemployed.

Here, he took Frances sightseeing, entertained her and his mother, and he learned everything he could about photography. He was a gifted painter, and his mother had lured him over to London so he could decide for himself if he wanted to spend his life with the "Top Note". He'd opened the night club because it offered him a chance to look after all the people he felt responsible for. Now he had well-trained staff to run it for him, Katherine had wanted him to have a chance to decide if he'd rather pursue his artistic dreams.

It had worked, she mused, as she reached for her bath sponge. As much as Jack loved painting - and in Frances's eyes he was every bit as good as the painters she'd seen exhibited in the National Gallery - he'd decided to use it and photography as relaxation from his real work. He'd been invited as a guest to a photographic society where he spent a few afternoons a week, intent on neglecting neither Frances nor his mother while they were in London.

As for herself - she heaved a tiny sigh. While Katherine seemed happy enough doing the shopping, supervising the daily help, volunteering in soup kitchens and organising charity raffles at her ladies' club, Frances had hardly anything at all to occupy her days. She didn't want to cling to Jack, or to Uncle Sal who had snagged a second small part in a talking picture. Who'd have thought that being a lady of leisure could lose its lustre so fast.

The maid had been deeply hurt at first when Frances insisted on tidying her and Jack's room herself, fearful her work wasn't up to scratch, until Frances explained she wanted to learn how to do things properly. Since she'd been in charge of the family home before she was twenty, she considered this a forgivable little white lie.

Occasionally she and Uncle Sal did the cooking, and she accompanied Katherine to the soup kitchen. That was the extent of her activities.

In Adelaide she'd return to her old job, or maybe take over office duties at the "Top Note", but here she found herself with too many idle hours. She'd read all the delightful P.G. Wodehouse novels, devoured Agatha Christie's bonzer crime stories and Katherine's ladies' magazines, and she spent hours writing letters home. The thin air mail sheets were expensive, but Frances had taken to combining several missives with the request to her mother to send or pass them on. This scheme satisfied Frances's frugal soul and allowed her to write as often as she had something of interest to tell, unless it had anything to do with solving crimes and chasing murderers. Those thrilling topics she chose not to touch upon, to spare her mum any unnecessary worry.

The water had cooled, and Frances hurried to towel off and wrap herself in her bathrobe. Layers of clothes and hot water bottles had become a major feature of her routine. She'd never complain about the Australian heat again, she decided.

By now, Leo was dry and cosy too. He'd curled up on a chair by the fireplace and snored gently. Katherine poured tea, and suddenly Frances felt ashamed about her restlessness. Everybody did their best to spoil her, and she should be grateful.

She smiled at her handsome husband, who buttered his second crumpet. "Weren't you going out, or did my rescue get in the way?"

"Nothing that can't wait," he said. "The sun's out again. If you want to, we could go feed the squirrels."

As if on cue, Leo opened one eye. Frances chuckled. Her fascination with the lively animals which were unknown in her native country, hadn't escaped anyone.

"Don't worry about me," she said. "You go and figure out your overexposure or whatever it is."

His mother patted his hand. "I'll borrow Frances, if that's allowed, and we'll see you at dinner?"

"Borrow me?" Frances perked up. Her mother-in-law, who'd divorced Jack's father before the war, thanks to generous Australian laws, and returned to England with her second husband, was always fun to be around.

"Unless you mind," Katherine said. "I could do with your assistance on a project we're working on at my club. Ladies only."

Jack's eyes crinkled at the corners. "Just let me know if you're getting into trouble and need my help."

Katherine arched a perfectly groomed eyebrow at him. "I assure you, darling, there is never any trouble at the Athena Club."

These words echoed in Frances's head as she trailed her mother-in-law into the club's large sitting room, only to see a pale young woman stuff something into her purse and crumple to the floor.

Chapter 2

"Sarah!" Katherine hurried to catch the woman. She caught her in her arms. "Please fetch the manageress, Frances," she said.

The reception area consisted of a desk with a visitor's log and a row of pigeonholes for mail behind it. Frances had expected to find the manageress or another staff member there. Instead, it sat empty.

Frances knocked on the office door adjacent to the reception. There was no reply. She knocked again and pressed the handle. The door swung open, just as a female voice behind her asked, "What can I do for you?"

Relief washed over Frances. "Katherine Parr sent me for help. There's a woman who seems to have fainted in the reading room."

The manageress, a capable looking woman of about forty years, with broad shoulders and a tidy if unfashionable bun at the nape of her neck, turned on her heel without further question. Her solid brogues and tweed costume reminded Frances of her former headmistress, who'd combined a kind heart with the strictness necessary to keep up discipline.

When they entered the sitting room, Katherine still knelt on the floor, with the patient's head in her lap.

"Open my handbag and pass me the bottle with smelling salts, please," she said to Frances, before she turned to the manageress. "Dorothy, is there an empty room or a sofa where Sarah can rest?"

"The bedrooms are on the first and second floor." The manageress chafed Sarah's wrists, while Frances wafted the smelling salts under Sarah's nose.

"That's a long way without a lift," Katherine said. She signalled Frances to stop and return the bottle to her handbag.

Frances eyed the small sofa. "We can put her on there and use a chair to prop up her feet."

"That should work," the manageress said. A hairpin slipped out of her bun.

Frances picked it up and handed it over.

"Thank you," the woman said as she rammed the pin home. "Sorry, I don't know your name. I'm Dot Lydell."

"Frances Pal - Sullivan, I mean." Frances pushed a chair into place, a little annoyed about the slip of her tongue. But then she'd lived for almost twenty-three years with her maiden name and a fortnight with her new one.

She added an extra cushion to the sofa..

Her mother-in-law took the stricken woman by the shoulders. Dot helped steer her, and then they deposited Sarah on the sofa, with her feet on the chair.. She'd come to by now, although her eyes were still glazed over, and her hands shook.

"She needs strong tea with sugar, and a few biscuits," Katherine ordered. "Take Frances to the kitchen and make sure we're not disturbed."

"I'll see to it," Dot said. For a fleeting moment Frances wondered why the manageress so easily accepted orders, but then again Katherine was used to decisive action, as a former suffragist.

Dot led Frances past a dining room with a long refectory table and into a serviceable kitchen where an elderly cook scrubbed the stove.

The kettle had just been boiled, and sugar bowl and biscuit tin stood ready.

Frances prepared a tray while Dot rushed off to talk to someone in a low voice.

In the reading room, Sarah sat up and gave Frances and Katherine a wan smile. "I'm so sorry to be such a nuisance. I have no idea what came over me." Her hand was painfully thin, and her eyes held a scared look.

Katherine soothed her. "Nonsense. Two spoons of sugar, Frances, dear."

They waited until Sarah had sipped the tea and nibbled a digestive. Slowly the colour returned to her cheeks. What must have been half a dozen other club members traipsed past the door, only to be turned away by a firm head shake from Katherine. Still, the haunted look in Sarah's eyes remained.

Frances remembered the paper Sarah had shoved into her pocket. It must have been bad news, she decided. "More tea?" she asked.

"Only if you have some too." Sarah swung her legs around to sit up properly. Her stockings had been carefully darned, and her shoes had been resoled, but her clothes were well made.

Like the Athena Club itself, Sarah had an air of quiet quality. Frances knew, or rather had been told by her mother-in-law, that most of London's clubs for women were either dedicated to the education of the lower classes or to the pursuit of arts and science.

Only a few, like this one, served as a happy medium, as a meeting place for women who were neither too high-brow nor lacking opportunities. It was the perfect place to get things done and not just talk about them as Katherine called it. During her years campaigning for the vote, she'd used it as headquarters to commandeer a small troupe of volunteers. Now, with the universal vote in place a quarter of a century after Australia, she focussed her energy on helping poor women and children.

Although Katherine hadn't struggled with real hardship, thanks to Jack's support of her and her second husband who'd been unemployed until recently, she possessed the same sense of social responsibility as her son.

They also shared the same ease of commandeering respect. So Frances wasn't surprised when Sarah let herself be told what to do. Only when Katherine asked her what set off the fainting spell did she hesitate.

Sarah's gaze flitted to the door.

Frances went and closed it properly.

Katherine wrapped her arm around Sarah's shoulders. "You can trust us. It's not - you're not ill?"

The only answer was a weak head shake.

"Would you like to go somewhere else?" Frances asked, sensing that a change of scenery might help calm down the still shaking woman.

Sarah gasped. "What time is it? I still need to do the shopping for our supper." She wiped her brow.

"You've got an hour until the shops close." Katherine frowned. "Why don't we take you to my place?"

"But the shopping - and Harold's supper — "

"Leave that to us. Frances, would you be so good as to fetch Sarah's coat and arrange for a taxi?"

Frances had to search a little until she found a maid, who took care of both requests. The Athena, while well frequented, was spread thin when it came to their staff. How lucky they were back home, where Jack made sure nobody overworked themselves in his service.

As Katherine had promised, they made one stop on their way home, at the fishmonger's. When their guest saw her plaice well-wrapped in her possession, she appeared calmer.

Once installed with more tea in the Parr's lounge, Frances put another log onto the fire, for comfort. The maisonette was quiet, with the men away and the maid already gone for the day.

She took a seat opposite Sarah, who sat quietly next to her hostess.

Frances took her to be in her mid-thirties, much younger than her own mother-in-law. Yet they seemed well acquainted.

"Whatever it is, my dear, it'll do you good to get it off your chest," Katherine said. "If it's not your health, what has upset you so badly?"

Sarah cast her eyes to the floor, as if the Turkish rug held important answers.

"You can trust us," Katherine repeated. "Haven't we been through enough together, when we campaigned for our rights?"

Frances saw Sarah in a different light now. This defeated looking woman must have more courage than she'd expected, to go by the reports of suffragists' clashes with police. Their marches and protests had demanded a lot of courage, even if they hadn't set out to change things violently, like their suffragette sisters.

"Please," Katherine said, "whatever it is, I promise I'll help you. Is it Harold? Or money?"

A well of tears erupted. "Nobody can help me."

"Try me."

Frances offered Sarah a handkerchief, to dry her face with.

"They'll say I'm a criminal," the woman whispered.

"What are you talking about? You'd never break the law, unless for a very good reason." Katherine gave Frances a questioning look.

Frances hoped she'd read the unspoken message correctly. "My husband is a lawbreaker," she said. "But only after six pm, when he's no longer allowed to serve alcohol to anyone but bona fide travellers. He runs a nightclub, so he has little choice than to ignore a law that's stupid in the first place."

"It's true," Katherine said. "Considering that for years my son helped Charles and me afford this home, and put food on our table, you might say we're all profiting from his creative attitude towards the South Australian law."

Sarah took a moment to digest this confession before she reluctantly put a crumpled envelope on the table. In typed letters, it was simply addressed to "Sarah Blake".

Katherine's brow furrowed. "That name is wrong."

"George Blake was my first husband." Fresh tears sprang into Sarah's eyes. "It's too horrible."

Frances longed to see the letter, if the very sight of simply the envelope could produce so much fear and pain in the poor woman. "Please don't think I want to pry, but do you mind if we read the message?"

For a second, Katherine looked at her aghast, before she nodded at Frances.

Silently, Sarah gave her permission.

Frances opened the letter. It consisted of only a few, typed lines. She read them out loud enough for Katherine to hear.

"Dear, dear wife,

thought you got rid of me, you and your fancy new man?

Think again and remember, till death do us part.

And while you live in clover, I barely have more than the shirt on my back. £50 would tide me over for a bit. I thought I'll ask you first, before I go and see your new man at his workplace.

Yours, forever,

George"

"Blackmail," Frances whispered as she dropped the letter. The simple act of reading it made her skin crawl.

"He was dead, Katherine, I swear. At least, I thought he was. Otherwise, I would have never — Harold mustn't know. Please." Sarah twisted her wedding band until Frances thought she'd rip it off her finger. "What if George gets him fired? Or if he goes to the police and says I'm a bigamist? I'll be thrown in prison."

"He won't dare, not while he's hoping for money," Frances said. "Are you sure this letter is really from your first husband?"

"There's no doubt. They said he was missing in action, and then I never heard another word. In March 1918 that was. But whenever George was mad or drunk, he used to remind me of my wedding vows. If only I'd never married him."

"Wouldn't he have been officially declared dead after a while? That should be proof of your innocence," Frances pointed out.

"I had to show that letter when I married Harold. But ..." Sarah fell silent.

"He could still cause a scandal, with or without an official document," Katherine said.

Sarah covered her eyes. "What do I do?"

Chapter 3

"There's only one thing," Frances. "We need to find him and make him stay away from you, unless you want him back."

"No, good lord, no. But he won't stay away from me, not George. And he's sure to raise hell if I don't do what he says."

"We need Jack, and Uncle Sal." Frances glanced at the wall clock. A quarter to six, so the men should be home soon.

Sarah's eyes widened in new fear. "Nobody else must find out."

"They won't tell a soul," Frances promised. "We've been involved in stickier situations before and always solved the problems."

"You?"

Frances grinned. "Maybe one day we'll tell you about one or two of our adventures."

"I'd like to hear about them." Katherine's eyes held a distinctive twinkle. "I did get the impression that Jack wasn't as forthright about a few things as he used to, and then there was your secrecy about how you came to be gifted your honeymoon."

Frances blushed. "We couldn't tell, and I'm only saying this now to show Sarah that she can trust us."

"Your Jack - what if he judges me, for not wanting my first husband to come near me, ever again? After all, George did serve in the trenches, and Harold didn't, with his home front job."

The log in the fireplace crackled as an amused voice said, "Why should I judge anyone?"

"Jack." Frances flung her arms around her husband. They'd been so immersed in Sarah's problem, they hadn't heard him come in. "I'm so glad you're back."

"I got that idea."

He bestowed a slow smile on Sarah as his mother introduced them. Frances could see their guest take stock of him, with his open features and the steady gaze from his blue eyes. Captain Jack, as his men sometimes still called him, had the knack of instilling trust in people.

His magic worked for Sarah, too, because she voluntarily showed him the letter.

He pondered it while his mother brought him a coffee.

Frances remembered Sarah's earlier urgency. "When is your husband coming home? Do you need to give him a buzz?"

"I've got to go. He'll be back by seven and if I'm not in the flat, or the dinner's not ready — "

"Ring him up and tell him there was an emergency at your friend's," Katherine suggested. "That's close enough to the truth."

"We don't have a private phone, and the landlady gets terribly cross if she's asked to go all the way up to our floor to deliver a message."

"Then you'll take the shepherd's pie that's sitting in our oven. It takes only twenty minutes to reheat it. You can make the plaice tomorrow."

Frances hurried to fetch the food, remembering in the last minute to check the pie dish was only lukewarm, before she burnt her fingers.

Her mind whirled. Surely there must be something they could do for poor Sarah, if they put their heads together.

Jack left them to pick up the car. The Parrs had no automobile of their own, but he'd purchased a secondhand Austin Twenty he kept in a garage nearby.

Although the long rows of Victorian houses held on to bits of their former glory, with their gables and stained-glass windows, crumbling mortar and chipped doors spoke of hardship. The drawn curtains in Sarah's lodging on the top floor were threadbare, Frances noticed as she and her mother-in-law saw her to the doorstep. How on earth anyone living here was to lay their hands on 50 pounds, she couldn't imagine.

Alone in her flat, Sarah's head felt light as she put the shepherd's pie in the oven. She'd given the letter to Katherine, for safekeeping, otherwise the fear of her husband discovering it would have driven her out of her mind.

Her husband! Her hands clutched at her throat. Yet, even if they lived in sin and had done so unwittingly for over a decade, Harold Todd was her husband, for better or worse. His quiet manner and gentleness had more than made up for every moment of misery she'd endured with George.

Her hands dropped. She ran her fingertips over a crescent-shaped scar on her wrist. She'd stumbled into the range in her clumsy attempt to evade George's fists when he'd roared home from the pub, all fired up with liquor and contempt for her.

Those moments she remembered in every single detail, although for the life of her she couldn't remember which of her actions had set him off.

The wall clock ticked away in a comforting manner. They'd created a nice home, she and Harold. The furniture gleamed with beeswax, and the piano Harold had given her as a wedding gift filled their living room with music every Friday night. She played her sheet music, and together they sang chorals and well-loved songs from their youth.

She sank onto a chair. She'd rather die than let anyone destroy their home. But how was she supposed to find £50? Her housekeeping money rarely left a couple of shillings in her purse at the end of a week.

A sob escaped her. No, she chided herself. She wouldn't give in to despair. Katherine had promised her help, and so had her young friend, or was it daughter-in-law? The young woman hadn't so much as flinched at the idea of Sarah's plight.

A key turned in the lock. "Something smells nice," Harold said as he hung up his hat and coat in the narrow hallway. He bent over to kiss her on the cheek, like he did every day after his return from work.

She squeezed his hand.

"You're pale, love." He peered at her in concern.

"It's nothing, only a spot of headache." Her pulse quickened. She'd never lied to Harold, until now. Yet what choice did she have, unless she was willing to destroy his own happiness together with her own?

Chapter 4

Frances watched the face of London change as they left the unassuming backwaters of Sarah's neighbourhood, with its small shops and children playing hopscotch on the roads. Drab buildings with front steps leading onto narrow pavements gave way to Victorian and Edwardian terraces with small stretches of lawn behind wrought-iron gates.

The people hustling along changed less. Constant cold and the worry of a hand-to-mouth existence left their marks on those too poor to afford a bus ticket or take the underground. In comparison, she and Jack were rich.

Behind her, in the comfortable backseat of the Austin, Katherine fidgeted. "You're going too fast."

"I'm not." Jack cast a concerned glance in the rear-view mirror. "It's unlike you to complain about speed."

"It's that poor woman. I can't think properly when I'm being all jolted about."

"We could all do with fresh air," Frances said.

"In London, in winter?" Jack teased her. It was true that a thick cloud of smoke hung constantly above the city as the chimneys belched. The smell of coal and wood was a constant reminder they were close to the factories and the East End.

"There must be somewhere we can walk for a spell," Frances said.

Jack directed the car towards Hyde Park. "Will a short stroll along the Serpentine do?"

He found a parking spot opposite one of the entrances to the park. An urchin ran up to them, to help Katherine out.

Jack handed the boy a sixpence. "If you guard the car for me, there's another half shilling in it for you."

"Cor blimey! You can count on me, guvnor." The boy bowed to Jack, and then Frances and Katherine with so much enthusiasm he had to hold on to his shabby cap.

Frances and her mother-in-law took Jack in their midst. The footpath along the Serpentine was muddy and stuck to their soles. They trod carefully in the near darkness. The park gates would soon close, but for now, they had the garden with its trees and water to themselves.

Frances drew a deep breath. She was still trying to familiarise herself with English trees and their scents. Oaks and firs and chestnuts were a far cry from the gum trees and eucalyptus of her native shores.

"Better?" Jack steered her away from a hole in the path.

"Much better." She beamed at him.

He asked his mother the same question.

"I'd say so, especially if you and Frances promise me we'll put our heads together and sort out Sarah's sad business."

"Too right we will," Frances said. "We'll start right after dinner."

A few stars fought their way through the smog. They twinkled above them as if they, too, wanted to show their support.

The urchin sprang to attention as they crossed the street. "I 'aven't let nobody touch yer bus, sir," he said.

"Excellent." True to his word, Jack rewarded him with half a shilling. Frances hoped the boy'd use the money for food, thin as he was, or to support his family.

Money. It was uppermost on most people's minds. Her thoughts returned to the blackmailer, and the problem at hand.

She mulled over the events of the afternoon when they'd retired to the drawing room after dinner. At Katherine's request they'd kept silent about the affair, to keep her husband out if it. Utterly trustworthy as he was, Sarah hadn't given them permission to spread the information still further.

The radio programme offered classical music - enough distraction to keep one part of Frances's brain occupied while the rest dissected what they knew.

"A penny for your thoughts," Jack murmured into her ear. "You have the same expression you wear when we're tracking down a criminal."

She whispered back. "Well, blackmail is a crime. And to do that to your own wife is abominable."

Katherine shushed them.

"We'll take Leo for a walk, so you two can listen in peace." Jack snapped his fingers at the puppy who ran straight to the drawer with his leash in it.

The headlights of a limousine pierced the mist, and faint lights shimmered through drawn curtains. Frances shoved her gloved hand deep into her pocket. With the other hand, she held Leo's leash. The dog sniffed every tree with the same deep satisfaction he'd demonstrated that morning, the day before, and all the other days.

Jack coaxed him away from a particularly fascinating oak, with a cat sitting in its branches.

He picked up their conversation. "From what I heard George didn't strike me as the kind of person who'd ever consider his wife's comfort, so threatening a scandal to extort money from her is no real surprise.

What I don't understand is why now, more than a dozen years after the war ended? She remarried a long time ago."

"Maybe he's only fallen on hard times lately," Frances said. "Although he seemed like the type who'd have raised hell over Sarah's taking up with another man before she had so much as the chance to exchange wedding vows."

"Which brings us to another interesting question. Where has he been all these years? Even if he was missing at one point, he seems to have picked up his life," Jack pondered. "I won't go into the details, but there'd be certain steps taken before a soldier was declared dead."

"Could he have had amnesia? Didn't that happen with certain head injuries? If he only recently got his memory back, that'd explain why it took him so long to get in touch."

"Possible, but not very likely. There would have been pictures in the newspapers, asking if anybody recognised the man, if he'd wandered around without remembering who he was. No, I think it much more likely that he was a deserter or wanted for some petty crime that made it impossible for him to show his face. There's a statute of limitations for certain felonies."

"Whatever happened, he's a coward alright, preying on poor Sarah." Frances huddled into her coat. "He's cornered her, hasn't he?"

"I'm afraid so. It wouldn't be the first case where a woman called herself a war widow to start over again. If this came to light, even if she had a sympathetic judge and jury who believed her story, she would be dragged through the newspapers and her second husband too."

"I said we'd help her." The puppy pulled at the leash, as a sign to Frances and Jack that he'd be willing to return to his spot in front of the fire for the night.

"We will. We'll come up with a plan tomorrow."

***

Frances woke early, with a sense of unease. Sarah's despair had haunted her half the night.

Breakfast took forever. Finally, with their host on his way to the office, Frances hoped for a quiet word with her mother-in-law, only to see Katherine occupied with discussing chores with the maid. It would have been so much easier for Frances to roll up the sleeves and do the dishes or run the duster across the surfaces.

How did rich people cope with the lack of privacy that came with having servants taking care of every aspect of their existence? At least at Aunt Mildred's, as she and Jack called their good friend, the Honourable Mrs Clifton, a closed door signalled to her small staff that any disturbance had better have an excellent reason.

Frances furrowed her brows. Aunt Mildred had recently inherited another title and was now officially Lady Mildred. What would her society chums say to her chumminess with a nightclub owner and a telephone exchange operator, not to mention an ex-Vaudevillian turned film extra? Uncle Sal carried himself like the true gentleman he was, but nobody could say that Frances's godfather, who was currently installed in Aunt Mildred's guest suite, had a single drop of blue blood in his veins.

Jack carried in a scuttle full of coals. The man who delivered them with an ancient vehicle gave Frances an apologetic bow. "You have to excuse me. The captain insisted on me taking a break."

The captain? Frances noticed the uneven clip of the man's step. Two fingers of his left hand missed the last digit.

"Frances, meet an old mate of mine, Sergeant Sam Finch. He's been in London since we were demobbed."

"How lovely to meet you. How do you do?" Frances shook Sam's hand with genuine pleasure. If there was anything good that had come out of the war, it was friendships and connections between people who otherwise would never have met.

Jack's network reached far and wide, apparently including the delivery driver of an East End coal merchant.

Sam grinned at her. "On top of the world, Ma'am. I can't wait to tell the missus who blew into town, and him newlywed, too."

Jack clapped him on the back. "We'll have a good old chinwag one of these days. Just give me a bell on this number." He slipped one of Katherine's calling cards into Sam's pocket.

The man's face lit up. "Right you are. You'll be amazed to see who else is around in these parts."

Outside, a car horn honked twice. "I'd better be off, before my customers complain to the boss." Sam gave Jack and Frances a quick salute.

Katherine rushed in as the door closed behind the veteran. "All sorted. If you, darling Jack, care to drop Frances and me off at Victoria Station, you're free to meet your photographer friend." She lowered her voice. "I've arranged to see Sarah in a place where you'd be noticed too much. She's frantic, poor thing."

"I'm at your command." He picked up his camera bag. "I'll fetch the car while you two put on your coats."

Frances waited until they were alone in the Austin before she asked, "Where are we going?"

"There's a soup kitchen, where Sarah and I both volunteer. She's a marvel at bookkeeping, so she spends most of her time in the tiny office, and it won't raise any suspicion if she slips out the back. There's a tea-room nearby that's run by an old friend, and she's promised me a secluded spot."

Chapter 5

Thus, five minutes after Jack had gone on to the photographic society, Frances followed Katherine and a stout woman with a maternal air up a creaking staircase, to a room overlooking the street. The woman clucked her tongue as she spotted a biscuit crumb under the large table. "That girl's never done her job properly, after the Sallies had their meeting. If you give me a sec, I'll get the carpet sweeper out."

"There's no need." Frances picked up the offending item and placed it in the wastepaper basket.

"I'll bring you a pot of tea and crumpets, while you wait. That'll warm you up." The woman switched on a small electric heater.

Katherine removed her gloves and hat but kept on her coat. Frances followed her example, to ward off the chill. Outside, buses sprayed rainwater from an earlier shower over the pavement, and the few people hurrying along.

Frances inspected her stockings. "Drat," she exclaimed as she tried to rub off a speck of mud with her tissue.

Katherine staid her hand. "It'll come out in the wash."

Hesitant footsteps could be heard on the creaking staircase.

Both women stood up to welcome Sarah.

A night's sleep hadn't restored her peace of mind, Frances assumed when she noticed how pale and haggard Sarah appeared in the harsh electric light.

The tea-room owner followed with a tray laden with buttered crumpets and strong tea. She deposited her load on the table and directed Sarah to the most comfortable chair. From a chest that doubled as window-seat, she produced a throw which she wrapped over Sarah's lap. "This'll warm you up in no time, love."

"Thanks." Sarah seemed to gather her strength. "I'm silly," she said as soon as they were alone. "I simply couldn't shake the sensation that I was being followed ... watched ... pursued."

"It's not silly at all under the circumstances," Frances said.

Her mother-in-law put a crumpet and cup of hot tea with two lumps of sugar in front of Sarah.

"The worst part is having to lie to my husband. I couldn't bear it if George were to approach him and spread falsehoods about me." A tear rolled down her cheek. She wiped it away with an angry movement. At least she had some fight left in her, Frances thought.

"Did you notice anyone watching?" she asked.

"No, but I was too scared to turn my head. It was all I could do to walk into the soup kitchen as if nothing had happened and dart out through the back."

"What I was wondering about is the letter. It was addressed to you, under your old name." Frances saw the envelope in her mind's eye.

"Yes."

"And you received it at your club?"

"We all have pigeon-holes there. It was stuck between a notice about changes to the annual fee and a ladies' magazine that gets passed around, from member to member. Everyone who has a subscription shares it with the rest of the ladies."

"Did the postman deliver it?"

Sarah gasped. "He didn't."

"Then whoever put it in your pigeon-hole must have done so personally or handed it to a member or the staff. How many people there know your old name?

"I didn't, for one," Katherine said. "And that despite being friends with you since my return from Australia, after the war."

"I never mentioned it. I wanted to forget all about him." A few drops of tea spilled out of Sarah's cup as she lifted it to her lips.

"I can't blame you," Katherine said. "I've rarely even thought about my first husband since the ink dried on my divorce papers." She flashed Frances a wry smile. "It may sound heartless, but it's the truth. I've done my best that my children didn't suffer too much, without a dad."

"From what Jack told me, you did the right thing." Frances shifted her attention to Sarah. "You do see how important it is to figure out how the letter arrived in your post?"

The woman pressed her fingertips against her temple. "If he went to the Athena once, he'll do it again. I don't think I could bear encountering him. Just the idea brings on another headache."

Katherine opened her handbag and took out a bottle with aspirin. She shook out two tablets. "Take these and you'll feel much more the thing."

"What if we go with you to the club?" Frances asked. "Do you have a routine?"

"Why, yes, most of us do. I go every Tuesday, when I run my errands and visit the fishmongers, and every second week for our charity meetings. Katherine attends them, too."

"There's a whole group of us, who met during or after the war. I was the last to join, when I returned home for good from Australia," Katherine said.

"Would someone notice if you had letters waiting for you?" Frances asked.

Sarah's brows knitted. "I don't reckon they would. The post area is between the manager's office and the reception desk. There's a potted plant blocking it from most of the light, too."

"It's an aspidistra, a hideous thing, but Dot's pride and joy," Katherine said.

"Does it matter?" Sarah asked.

"Well, if nobody'd pay attention, the letter might have been slipped into your pigeon-hole any time since your last visit. If on the other hand people would spot the post, then an envelope using your old name surely would set tongues wagging. Maybe if Katherine tried to pick up some gossip ..." Frances bit her tongue as she saw the rising fear in Sarah's face. "Without mentioning you, of course. You must see how important this is."

Blank stares answered her.

"Otherwise, it's highly likely that George knew your routine well enough to arrange the arrival of his letter with precision," she explained.

Sarah swayed. "He's been watching me this whole time? Maybe he's spying on Harold too, waiting for the right moment?"

Katherine took her hand and chafed it. "Don't think that. He wouldn't dare approach your Harold, not if he hopes to extort money from you. Otherwise, he'd already have done it, to hurt you." She took a monogrammed flask from her purse and poured a generous dose of an amber liquid into a glass. "Drink this."

Frances sniffed. "Brandy?"

"A gift from Jack. He told me to carry it with me for all eventualities."

How typical. Happiness spread through Frances's body. He'd given her brandy too, to ward off shock, when they first became acquainted. It had worked then, and it worked now.

A little colour returned to Sarah's cheeks as she sipped the liquid. She coughed. "That's strong."

"What do we do next?" Katherine asked.

"We wait for the next letter," Frances said.

"The next one?"

"There has to be another letter, doesn't it? One with instructions where and how to pay. Because there was nothing of the sort in the first one."

Sarah cried out. Katherine shushed her. "It'll be fine."

"But how? I might as well throw myself off a bridge to end this misery."

"Don't say that. Don't even think it. You've done nothing wrong, nothing at all." A dozen ideas ran through Frances's head, only to be discarded in an instant.

She needed Jack to talk things through, and Uncle Sal. Together they'd solved harder problems than this. The important thing now was making sure that Sarah didn't do anything desperate.

Chapter 6

J ack wandered around the photographic exhibition. One part of his brain admired the juxtaposition of light and darkness in a series of pictures from the docks next to images from the concert halls. Fur-wrapped society ladies, bright young things in revealing evening frocks and draped around men in tuxedos, hung next to portraits of street vendors hawking anything people might pay a penny for.

The sepia tint or stark black and white matched the mood. Back in Australia, whatever the season, the colours were so much more vibrant and vivid that it took an effort to remember they were real.

The bigger part of his brain was occupied with recent events. He hadn't told Frances, or his mother, in case he was wrong. Yet deep down he saw no easy way out.

The blackmailer was after more than just money. Anyone could see it would take a miracle for Sarah to come up with £50. Instead of starting with a reasonable amount and then tightening the thumbscrews, George had started with a moonshot, one that would cause Sarah to sell or pawn everything she could.

Then there was the added pressure of letting her wait for more communication.

George wasn't only a blackmailer. His actions spoke of sadism and a deep-rooted hatred of the woman he'd married and mistreated. He'd want to see her suffer for as long as possible. And there was nothing to stop him from falsely accusing her in public of having known he wasn't dead. Nothing, unless Jack found a way to prevent that.

"Great angle, eh?" a man next to him said. He put his hands together to form a frame through which he looked at the picture. "Gives you a whole new perspective."

"It does," Jack said.

The man proffered his hand. "You're a photographer too, right? I've seen you around before. Roderick Shelby, at your service."

"Jack Sullivan." They shook hands.

"Any of these yours?" Shelby asked.

"I wish." Jack cast a longing glance at the nightclub scenes. If he could capture the essence of the Top Note like this, or of Adelaide with its good and bad sides, it might be what he was searching for.

"Those are mine," Shelby said, pointing at Jack's favourites. "Not bad, if I say so."

"How did you approach this? Do you ask permission?" Jack's gaze fastened on a couple of bright young things climbing into a fountain. The woman's head was thrown back, and Jack very much suspected that she and her companion were fuelled by more than champagne and legal stimulants.

The photographer chuckled. "That's a tricky one. I wouldn't advise anyone to dash out with their photographic apparatus, but so far nobody has complained. See how I make sure their faces are a little obscured? I'm a member of the press, too, in case there's some noise. If you plan to take your camera on a little outing, it pays off not to use too bright flashlight or you'll blind your subjects." He beckoned Jack over to a table with several large photographic albums.

Rifling through one, he lifted the tissue paper off a page. It showed a young man, staring wildly ahead in one picture and shielding his eyes in the next. "Caught like a deer in the headlights. If it's a celebrity

or aristocrat doing something they shouldn't it's one thing, but this
fellow'd only dropped off a message to a certain lady. So, you need to
have your facts straight, before you go a-hunting."

"Fair enough."

"Shelby?" Another man called out.

"On my way." The photographer closed the album. "Here's my
card, if you want another chat."

Jack slid it in his pocket and left with more than enough food for
thought.

***

At the tea-room Katherine urged Sarah to finish her crumpet.
"You'll need all the strength you can muster. And so do we."

Frances admired the ease with which her mother-in-law took charge
without being overbearing. Jack resembled her in so many ways.

Their guest hastened to eat the last bites. "If he's watching, he
might wonder what takes me so long, usually my shifts only last two
hours."

"We still have a few minutes left," Frances said. "Do you think we
could go into the soup kitchen and bump into you there? Then we
could accompany you to the club."

"I'm not sure that's a good idea. What if he notices me going on the
wrong day? And in company, too."

Katherine chimed in. "Nonsense. Frances is right. If anything, he'll
think you're anxiously waiting for the next communication. As for
company, if George keeps you under surveillance, he'll have seen me
with you before. Nothing suspicious about that."

Sarah didn't seem convinced but at least she gave in.

The weather was too foul for walking. Frances regretted the lost opportunity to see if they were being followed, and maybe catch a glimpse of that brute. On the other hand, Sarah already struggled enough with her fear of him.

They squeezed onto seats on the upper deck of a bus towards the Athena Club. Sarah gripped her handbag so hard her knuckles turned white.

"When is your husband expecting you back?" Katherine asked.

"I need to be home by afternoon teatime, to make supper."

"We'll have you back long before that."

Again, the reception desk sat empty while Dot dealt with an issue in the kitchen, judging by the faint voices Frances heard.

The pigeon-holes for the mail all carried individual brass tags with the name of the owner. They must have been expensive, Frances thought. The whole club spoke of a former quiet affluence with its numerous rooms for eating, entertainment and quiet studies, and two floors dedicated to members' bedrooms.

She scanned the scene from different angles. Like Sarah had told them, from most vantage points, the aspidistra cast a large shadow over the wall with the pigeon-holes. It would be easy to slip a letter into Sarah's slot or indeed most of the others, without being noticed. They were large and deep enough to easily fit a magazine, and she had to peer closely to spot anything inside all but the most prominent four slots.

Katherine's pigeon-hole held a notice about an upcoming meeting. From the two yards distance between reception desk and wall cubicles, Frances had been unable to spot it.

She glanced around. The other side of the hallway was taken up by two rooms, one for meetings, the other served as a separate lounge for residents. The upper part of the door was made of milky glass. If only there was a way to observe the reception area! Although Frances struggled to believe that George had an accomplice, it appeared plausible that he'd pay someone to enter the lion's den and drop off his blackmail letters. A sixpence would secure the services of any number of men or boys on the streets.

But even then, he'd probably be watching, which might lead them to his lodgings. That kind of information could be used to turn the tables on George, if he didn't leave Sarah alone after she'd paid.

That Sarah would part with all her savings, Frances didn't doubt. She wondered if in the same situation, she'd dare risk slander – and that's what it was, evil slander - becoming public knowlegde. The very idea made her stomach knot.

The manageress hurried through the kitchen door, towards them. "I'm so sorry I always seem to be rushing around like a headless chicken these days. It's one crisis after another." She wiped her hands on an apron.

"What is it this time? Anything we can help you with, my dear?" Katherine asked.

"That's very kind of you, but really, it's nothing, only our upstairs maid fell ill, and now the kitchen maid has come down with flu, so I had to give cook a hand."

"What a shame. I hope the girl recovers soon. You're already short-staffed as it is."

Dot shrugged. "I don't believe in draining our coffers if we don't have to or raising the member's fees. Our bedrooms upstairs are the only chance most of our far-flung ladies have to visit the capitol."

"How do you keep the club so nice?" Frances asked. "It's like a palace, compared to Australia." Inwardly, she begged her hometown for forgiveness. Adelaide might be remote and young, but it had its fair share of mansions and elegant art nouveau buildings fit for a lord.

"Our late patroness, Lady Pemberton, may she rest in peace, left us the freehold and a yearly stipend that a decade ago was more than sufficient for the upkeep and a staff of a dozen. Nowadays though - I've done my best to trim our sails in these difficult years, but it's not easy. A small, dedicated staff, that's the Athena's backbone, that and our members. We're all accustomed to pitching in, aren't we?"

"As long as you know you're welcome to ask for assistance whenever you need it," Katherine said.

"I appreciate it."

A cry from the kitchen alerted Dot to a possible new crisis. "You must have a bad impression of us," she said to Frances. "I promise, normally everything in these four walls runs as smooth as silk."

"I don't doubt it."

As Dot dashed off, a man in work clothes touched the brim of his cap to greet her from the washroom. "The sink's all fixed." From upstairs came faint carpet sweeping noises.

"Are these all employees?" Frances asked Katherine in a low voice.

"They've been here for years. The laid-up maid is the newest addition, and she started two years ago. Her big sister's in service with one of the other ladies."

It all sounded almost like the Top Note, where Jack employed men who'd served under his command, or their family members.

The doorbell rang in a staccato.

"Billy, could you take care of it?" Dot called out. "It must be our guests from Norwich."

"He's employed as the man," Katharine explained. A sturdy man in work clothes gave Frances, Katherine, and Sarah a respectful nod as he headed towards the door. "Ma'am."

"We should be going," Katherine said.

They passed two fortyish women in identical tweed and brogues. Their hair was scraped back into severe buns, and the luggage that the man carried consisted of battered suitcases and sturdy umbrellas. A lively twinkle in their eyes and luggage labels from hotels in Torquay and Deauville stood in contrast to their staid appearance.

"I hope we'll have our usual rooms," one of them said to the man. The other one waved at Katherine. "Will we see you at the annual meeting?"

"Dash and Poppy, as I live and breath! I wouldn't miss it for the world."

On their way to the bus stop, Katherine said, "Don't let those weird nicknames fool you. They're short for balderdash and poppycock. Legend has it, half the men in Westminster and Whitehall trembled when the sisters uttered those words. Those two gals trained half the suffragists and suffragettes in their county in jiu-jitsu. They taught me too."

"It seems like an eternity ago," Sarah said, as they saw her onto her bus, but a weak smile flitted over her face.

Katherine pecked her on the cheek. "Together we'll always prevail. Remember, if we don't show the world we deserve respect, nobody else will show it to us."

The bus doors closed.

Katherine twinkled at Frances. "I'm convinced my son won't need to be reminded of that, but not many men had his upbringing."

"Uncle Sal's the same. He'd rather go hungry himself than have me or my mum make any sacrifices."

"Birds of a feather. And now your Uncle Sal's a budding star in the talkies."

Chapter 7

The budding star waited for Jack and Frances in the drawing room of his hostess's mansion. If he had any qualms about his extended stay under Aunt Mildred's roof, he hid them well. As for her society chums, they probably paled in comparison to the dapper "Salvatore the Magnificent" as he was called on the Vaudeville stage.

Frances wondered which name would appear on the cinema screen. Or did only the actors with big parts receive billing?

"Mildred will be down in a jiffy," he said. "Shall we wait with our cocktails?"

"Yes, please. You've become very fashionable, haven't you? With pre-dinner drinks and all?" Frances beamed at her godfather. Uncle Sal deserved his good fortune, and these luxurious surroundings. A car accident caused by a boozed-up driver had cut his stage career short, and only since they met Jack had he been able to perform once in a while. Yet none of the actors, stage-magicians and other artists she'd seen in the London theatres could compete with his flair.

They sat around the fireplace. Its flames filled the room with homely sounds and much appreciated warmth.

An excited yap announced corgi Tinkerbell, and his doting mistress. Frances half wished they'd brought their puppy. Still, Leo would be fast asleep in his own basket, next to Katherine, while in the background the wireless or the gramophone played.

"Frances, my dear, and Jack." A soft powdered cheek touched Frances's. Aunt Mildred's familiar scent of tuberose lingered for an instant in Frances's nostrils. Like everything else about the unflappable society lady, her perfume was subtle yet memorable. "We don't see you nearly often enough."

"You're only saying that because you're too polite to fob me off to your butler to help me with my rehearsals." Uncle Sal chuckled.

So did Aunt Mildred. "As if I'd ever tire of the excitement. The artistic life is so much more fun than discussing match-making strategies with ambitious mamas and grandmamas."

"Rehearsals? I thought the director was in charge of that."

"Well, yes and no. There're enough folks only too happy to put on their glad-rags and cross in front of the cameras, but that's not me. If I act, I need to inhabit the part." He took the cocktail shaker and filled it with various liquids. "If I'm an experienced drinker, or bartender, I'll shake it like this." He demonstrated a few quick, confident shakes. "If I'm new to the whole scene, it'd look like this." He demonstrated this, too. "Or if I'm the villain, planning to drug the damsel in distress or the underworld king..." He seemed to notice something scary in the corner by the fireplace. Frances's gaze travelled into that direction until she stopped herself at the last moment. If she'd allowed herself to be distracted any longer, she'd have missed Uncle Sal's pretending to add something to the shaker in a sleight of hand.

"Bravo," she said.

"Now you see what I mean." Aunt Mildred pointed at the liquor cabinet. "Although I hope you didn't only use this to prove your point."

"Would I ever?" Uncle Sal filled four glasses with a golden liquid. "Don't worry, Franny, it's only a dash of champagne added to it. Hodges gave me the recipe."

"It's a rare honour. My esteemed butler is stingy when it comes to his secrets."

The cocktail tasted sublime, with hints of fruit and yet enough tartness to prevent it from being sweet.

The dinner gong sounded as they finished their drinks.

During the meal, Uncle Sal regaled them with his tales from the film word. He'd been asked to audition for another part, one that included several scenes with the hero and heroine. Tinkerbell lay curled up, his belly full of chicken. His blissful sighs added to the peaceful atmosphere.

Frances waited until they dug into their bread-and-butter pudding, which had been added to the menu as a special treat for her, before she mentioned Sarah's plight.

Uncle Sal and Aunt Mildred listened in silence, their expression changing from concern to disgust. They were so in tune, their reaction mirrored each other, Frances noticed. Who'd have thought that a stage entertainer who'd learned his letters and sums backstage in the music halls of old and a British aristocrat had so much in common?

"What a horrible thing," Aunt Mildred said at the end of the story. "If I can be of any assistance, I'd be only too glad to help."

"There are a few things," Frances said. "Uncle Sal, how would you approach the blackmailer as a character, if you were to play him?"

"Crawl under his skin, you mean?" Uncle Sal pondered the question.

"Exactly. We need to understand him if we want to outwit him. I've got another question for you, Aunt Mildred. How does a ladies' club really work?"

"That depends on the establishment," Aunt Mildred said.

"A club like the Athena." So far, Frances had omitted using any names. That way she and Jack could be as discreet as possible while still seeking advice.

"Virginia Pemberton's pet project?"

"You knew her?" It shouldn't have come as a surprise. As big as London was, certain circles were small and tightly knit.

"She was a sweetheart. Formidable, too. She cared very much about women's advancement. Her own parents had been mortified when their only daughter showed unfeminine ambitions and insisted on studying Latin and astronomy with a private tutor, instead of marrying during her first season."

"She went to university?" Was that a pang of envy she felt? Frances had always been content with her education, and her ability to earn enough money to keep a roof over their head and support her mother. Learning for leisure was a concept as alien to her as, well, the world they now moved in courtesy of Aunt Mildred.

"Heavens, no. Sadly." Aunt Mildred's lips pressed together. "There wasn't universal access to the colleges back then, but when she did get married, her husband was only too happy to supply her with the best teachers. Her family cut her off when she tied the knot with a wealthy merchant who was a patron of the astronomer's society."

"She must have been remarkable," Jack said.

"She was a generation older than me, but she never tired of her interest in good causes. Her husband died shortly after being made a peer, and she threw herself into the idea of suffrage and then, a club where women with common interests could meet or stay."

"Like former war nurses and suffragists?"

"There are other institutions aiming to instruct working class girls, or where bright young things bored of partying try to slum it with the poor, but Virginia Pemberton wanted to fill a gap, I suppose. She died while the Athena was in its infancy."

"My mother had to give two character references from women of good standing before she was accepted as a member," Jack said. "How much personal information would be requested when you join?"

"Not much more than that. Although I assume any woman considering herself to be widowed wouldn't have thought twice about stating her married name in the register and then updating it. I assume that's what you were wondering about?"

"I was," Frances said. "Although I don't really know why. After all, Geo- the first husband was sure to have all this information."

"He would. The question is, if the wife remarried over a decade ago, how did he find her? Unless she stayed in her old neighbourhood?" Aunt Mildred asked.

"That's a very good question," Jack admitted. "It's also one I intend to answer. It would be interesting to hear if anyone from his old battalion has heard about his recent reappearance."

"Someone like Sam Finch, maybe?" Frances addressed Aunt Mildred and Uncle Sal. "He's one of Jack's old veteran mates who delivers coal to the Athena Club and other addresses in the area."

"Someone like him could've recognised the missus of an old mate and mentioned to the cove that he'd seen a lady who was the spitting image of her," Jack said. "Not Sam himself, most likely, but someone in a similar position."

"That's a reasonable explanation." Uncle Sal hunched his shoulders. His eyes slitted and for a heartbeat, Frances had trouble recognising him. He'd become another, shiftier character. "Can we give him a name? It helps me get under his skin."

"It's George." It was a common enough name.

"George. The way I see it, he's a coward." He changed back to his normal self.

"Because he sent a letter instead of confronting Sarah and demanding money?" Frances asked, glad to hear he shared her opinion.

"What I'd like to know is where he was all these years," Aunt Mildred said, echoing Jack. "Simply hiding somewhere? And why?"

"Fear of some sort of prosecution is the likeliest explanation, so he had to wait until that danger was over. Jack and I talked about it," Frances said.

"I don't see how. The British law doesn't really allow for a statute of limitations," Uncle Sal said to Frances's surprise. "One of the other bit actors told me. He'd been close to starring in a picture that was scrapped when the studio lawyer pointed out that a wanted embezzler, who'd promised to cough up the money, couldn't just wait out the law."

"What if only one person could bring charges against George and that person died recently? Then he'd think himself safe," Jack said.

"That's plausible. Although I don't understand why he didn't start his demands lower, say at a couple of quid a week. That'd be enough to live on and the poor woman might be able to pay," Uncle Sal said.

"Unless he had to disappear again, fast," Aunt Mildred pointed out.

Frances shook her head. "Then he'd have given his wife instructions on how to pay." She sighed. "If only I could take a post as maid at the Athena Club, then I could observe comings and goings. But I've been introduced as Katherine's daughter-in-law, so that's no use. And they already employ a man, so Jack can't go undercover either."

"You believe the club is the important factor? I could try to become a member but I'm afraid I'd stick out too much." Aunt Mildred sounded rueful. Tinkerbell raised his head and gave a gentle woof. She reached out her hand and he ran up, to drop himself at her feet.

"I think the club's our best chance." Frances had discussed the issue with Jack. "Hopefully that's where the next letter will arrive. He won't risk sending it to her marital home, where the new husband might open it. If we can't trace the letter back to him and make him stop, she'll never feel safe again."

"Only, how can you end this?"

"Your connections," Frances said. "Maybe Sir Reginald Fitzpatrick could help. He's still in government intelligence, isn't he? If he threatens George with prison, for blackmail, I'm sure that'd be enough." Aunt Mildred's old friend held an important, if shadowy position. They'd met in in France, at Aunt Mildred's New Year's party, when they'd all been instrumental in assisting him unofficially on a case of espionage and murder, so Frances knew him to be trustworthy and resourceful.

"That's a promising idea," Aunt Mildred agreed.

"If we can locate the bastard," Uncle Sal said.

"We will. We have to." Frances gazed around. If anyone was capable of finding a way out of this mess, surely it was them.

Chapter 8

Sarah dreaded leaving her home. Doing so much as running simple errands like picking up the laundry or going to the greengrocer's took all her resilience. With every step she took outside she felt herself watched, judged, threatened.

Harold had become so concerned about her that he'd suggested a visit to her doctor.

She dragged herself out of the front door. Every single step thudded in her ears, together with the too loud beating of her heart. She daren't glance back, for fear of who she might see. Yet she constantly listened if there was any footfall echoing hers, as from a stealthy follower.

"Are you alright, love?" A woman she'd never seen before clasped Sarah's arm to steady her, as she stumbled.

"I'm fine, thank you." Where had the woman come from? Was she connected to George? Did he have others spying on her too? A sob escaped her. She needed to pull herself together.

At the end of the road stood a public telephone box. She'd ring up Katherine before she lost her mind.

"You poor thing." Katherine bundled Sarah in a taxi.

"My groceries." At the last instant, Sarah remembered the shopping she'd done while she waited for Katherine.

"Here you go, love." The shopkeeper hurried towards them, with a bag full of cabbages, onions, and potatoes. She gave Katherine, and the taxi, a curious look. "Something wrong?"

Sarah managed a wan shake of her head.

"She'll be telling the whole street about this," she fretted as the driver set off.

"Never mind." Katherine took out her powder compact. It held a small mirror. It allowed her to ensure they weren't followed. That should ease Sarah's mind a little.

"Where are we going?" Sarah asked as the driver turned towards Hampstead Heath.

"To see old friends."

They arrived at an old warehouse that had seen better days. The windows on the upper floors were grimy and the name plate was illegible with rust and dirt. Yet Sarah's face lit up. "Our old headquarters."

"The sisters told me you all used to meet here before the war."

Frances already waited for them inside. She was kneeling on an old sack and busy scrubbing out a large room at the back. It smelled faintly of machine oil, but the floorboards were well-kept. "I'll be done in a jiffy and then we can roll out the mats."

"What's going on?" Sarah asked.

"I've asked Dash and Poppy to give Frances a few lessons in jiu-jitsu and mentioned that you and I wouldn't mind a refresher ourselves. You'll feel a lot calmer once you remember what you're capable off."

"I hope so." Sarah wrung her hands. "It's this constant waiting and wracking my brain where the money's supposed to come from. A whole 50 pound! He might as well demand the moon."

"Don't worry about that now," Katherine said.

Frances held her tongue. She understood only too well how impossible it would be not to worry. She'd been the sole breadwinner for herself and her mother since she turned 19. Yes, Katherine had lived in reduced circumstances, yet Jack had ensured that she never had to encounter real hardship.

"He'll be aware of that," Frances said. "You could slip a note in your pigeon-hole, offering to pay him in instalments."

"I could." Sarah took a deep breath.

"It's worth a try. Otherwise, we could supply the money. Jack would do it," Katherine said.

"Only, what's George going to think or do if Sarah readily has access to a small fortune?" What Frances kept silent about was the idea of tracking down George. One payment would offer them only one chance.

Outside, the heavy knocker banged twice on the metal door.

Frances and Sarah heaved large mats out of an old cupboard and spread them on the floor. A few carried what looked suspiciously like small blood stains. "That's where I gave my teacher a nosebleed," Sarah said with an almost wistful glance at the rust-coloured spot. "I'd flailed so much I accidentally hit Poppy with my elbow."

The sisters strode in, and the whole atmosphere changed. Poppy and Dash took turns, bellowing orders and doling out gentle encouragement. What they both didn't allow was an instant's hesitation, when it came to following their instructions.

An hour later, Frances collapsed on a chair, catching her breath. Her muscles ached, yet she also felt exhilaration surging through her veins. Woe the attacker who dared cross paths with the sisters or their students. They'd all taken turns acting as assailant and victim. No, victim was the wrong word. The secret to this self-defence technique lay in using the other person's body weight and momentum against them, which favoured the women.

Already, Sarah held her head higher and a sparkle had returned that told Frances about the real woman hiding in the scared person she'd met.

"A few more sessions and we'll have you licked into shape," Dash declared. Her left hand carried a scar on two fingers, looking like an old cut from a knife. That was the only distinction between the two Frances had discovered.

"You haven't forgotten any of the tricks." Sarah panted.

"Once a week we train the girls at the Women's Institute. Can't have anyone take advantage of us, now, eh?"

"We're also in charge of the cricket team. Ten matches in a row without defeat!" Poppy said. "And we're fighting to have women's football reinstated. Poppycock to have it being banned for a decade when thousands used to come to see the gals play."

"Balderdash," her sister added. "You ladies go and see your local member of parliament and tell them what's what. Can't have them turn back the clock on us, can we?"

"We will," Katherine promised.

Dash slapped the cupboard where the mats had been stored. "This brings back fond memories. I wish you'd been there, Katherine, when the bobbies tried to round us up and drag us to the police station to be booked for unrest."

Frances gaped. "Why would they do that?"

Dash and Poppy chuckled. "Bless your innocence, sweetheart. The men fought us tooth and nail to keep us women down, but we got the vote in the end. You've no idea how lucky you Australians have it."

Frances beamed. Whenever she felt a little outclassed or overwhelmed with England's history and grandeur, all it needed was to remind her that Australia in a way was much more modern and tolerant than the old world. Voting rights were something she'd never had to fight for, and neither did her mum. Margaret Palmer had been allowed to cast her vote since long before Frances was born.

Their upbeat mood lasted even after the sisters had left. Sarah showed Frances another move which was useful to throw off an attacker. "It really works, even if you're up against a brute twice your size."

"You had to use it for real?"

Sarah nodded her confirmation. "Once, just before the war. George had been taken to hospital. His appendix was fit to bursting, they said, and he sent me home to bring him his shaving kit and a fresh set of clothes. It was late when I'd dropped everything off for him, and I had to hurry to catch my bus. There was a shortcut, through an alley." She paused. "If it hadn't been for Dash and Poppy and their lessons, I might not be here today."

"How fortunate that George didn't stop you from attending those classes. You must have some good memories," Frances said.

"I didn't tell him. I copped a black eye when he found out. Uppity females, poisoning my mind, that's what he said." She straightened her shoulders. "I can't believe he's back to torment me, after all these years."

"He underestimated you then, and he underestimates you now." Katherine linked arms with Sarah. "Your worries will soon be behind you."

Chapter 9

F og swirled around the streetlights as Jack reached The Crown and Anchor. Inside the pub, a dozen men in workers' clothes stood around a dart board. The floorboards were sticky with spilt beer. The bartender polished the wooden counter, where countless rings had left indelible stains. He had an apron tied around his waist. His balding hair was slicked back.

"What can I do for you?" he asked Jack.

"A pint of bitter."

"Coming right up."

While the bartender poured the bitter, Jack scanned the room. None of the other guests were known to him, but he assumed they came here most nights, for a drink and company, and to escape the cold. In the hearth blazed a cheerful fire, and a full coal scuttle promised ample warmth.

"I haven't seen you around before." The bartender put Jack's glass on a coaster.

"I'm visiting family. Is Sam Finch around?"

The bartender stood a little straighter. "You serve with him? The door on the right leads through to the saloon. That's where you'll find your mates."

"Much obliged." Jack picked up his drink and the coaster.

A solid baize door muffled the noise from the bar. The saloon had its own serving area, with a blackboard announcing beer on tap, sherry, tea, and coffee. On any other evening, this area was open to women and families. Tonight, it was reserved for the veterans. A small wooden plaque on the wall commemorated the war and those who hadn't returned.

Jack had hoped for names, or at least the mention of battalions, to given him an opening, but there was no list added. Ah well, he'd come up with something.

"Captain Jack." Sam jumped up from his seat. Three tables had been shoved together, to accommodate 14 men. They all shared the hard worn look of people used to graft and bad luck, while still holding their heads high.

"Lads, this is Captain Jack Sullivan, all the way from Australia."

"That's a mighty long trek just for a decent pint." One of the men, a sprightly Cockney with a raspy voice said. The men chuckled.

Jack joined in. "I was born in London, and my mother lives here."

"How are you finding the Big Smoke these days?"

"Still a sight for sore eyes. Round of the usual okay for you gentlemen?" Loud cheers confirmed his suggestion.

Behind the saloon bar, an elderly man Jack took to be the father of the barkeeper he'd met, sprang into action.

Jack dropped some money onto the counter.

"You can run a tab here," the man said. "Seeing as Sam vouches for you."

"That's very generous but I prefer to stay on top of my bills. I've had enough jokers trying to stiff me when I started out with my own place."

The man helped Jack carry the pints.

"You've got a pub at home?" he asked as they served them around.

Jack sensed renewed scrutiny, mixed with admiration. He'd carefully selected his suit for tonight. It was well-worn, yet of good quality and should inspire the confidence that Jack was doing well enough, without being worlds apart from the men in the saloon bar. They'd probably seen more than enough toffs and snotty upstarts ordering them around to last them a lifetime.

"A night club. Adelaide's not the biggest city, but we're doing well enough. It helps that I got to stick with the men I served with."

"Makes me almost wish I'd gone back with you, Captain Jack." Sam helped himself to a pint. He took a deep swig. "Except the missus wouldn't leave her old folks, not for a thousand quid."

"You're lucky with your old ball and chain." The man with the raspy voice grabbed a drink. "Mine's a proper harridan if I so much as trudge in a bit of mud when she's been scrubbing."

"At least she's still around," another man said. Shrapnel scars had left him with an immobile face. "Not like some I could name."

"Boys, boys," Sam admonished. "We don't want to give Captain Jack the impression we're nothing but a bunch of hen-pecked blokes, and him just hitched himself to a nice young lady."

As much as he'd have loved to stay on the topic, Jack decided to hold his tongue. If he managed to put the men at ease, it was a good start. He started asking after the local rugby team.

He left The Crown and Anchor after another couple of rounds, with the satisfaction of having been accepted as one of their own and being invited back to join them again. He'd also made notes which regiments his new friends had served in.

As big as London was, veterans knew each other, and when they got together, they let their tongues wag. Things they'd never confide even to their nearest and dearest were fair game to tell someone who'd shared the same hell.

A solitary light burned in the house when he returned. Frances was waiting up for him, with the puppy. She stifled a big yawn. "Katherine's left the kettle on the gas ring, if you want a cup of tea."

"Not this close to midnight." He picked up the dog. "Has he been out for a last walk?"

"Before Katherine went to bed." She yawned again. Her eyes fluttered shut.

"Go to bed. I'll only take a few moments."

"Good." Half asleep, Frances headed for bed.

Leo gave him a hopeful look. Jack stroked him. "We'll go to the park after breakfast."

***

"I've been thinking." Frances decapitated her boiled egg. "We can't drop into the club every day without it looking funny. So, if we want to keep watch on those pigeon-holes, we need to figure out exactly what's happening when."

"Too many questions might backfire, which is why I have to tread carefully with Sam," Jack said.

"True. I've got another idea, one that leaves us out of it." She spread marmalade onto her toast and took a big bite.

Katherine frowned. "The maid will be back from her errands in a few minutes. Either you tell us now or she might overhear us."

"It's very simple, really." Frances took her delight in watching their impressed faces as she told them what she'd come up with.

Chapter 10

Katherine and Frances were enjoying tea in the lounge with Dash and Poppy, when the manageress rushed in, with a flushed face and all signs of agitation. She panted as she closed the door although her office lay only a few yards away. Why was she out of breath? Frances wondered.

Dot's gaze swivelled around wildly. It fell onto a few crumbs on the floor. They were all that was left of cook's excellent crumpets which, on a chilly day, had been most welcome.

"What's wrong, my dear?" Poppy peered at her with deep concern. "Shall we ring up a doctor."

"It's nothing of the sort. Only, I had a phone call from a dear friend of Lady Pemberton's. She'll be here in a few minutes."

"What an honour," Frances exclaimed.

"It is, only how on earth am I going to look, with crumbs and dust everywhere and only half the rooms made up?" Dot talked herself into a tizzy.

"It can't be that bad," Katherine declared.

"The upstairs maid's still not fit to return to work." Bright circles formed on Dot's cheeks. "I'd send up Billy to tackle the rooms, only it wouldn't seem right, with this being a ladies' club."

Loud bangs from the boiler room demonstrated the man's presence.

"We'll help," Katherine said. "It's the least we can do for the Athena."

"Katherine's right. If you show us to the duster and carpet sweeper, we'll have the lounge ship-shape in the shake of a lamb's tail." Dash collected the used tea things. "I'll take these to the kitchen."

"Frances and I'll dust your office and the reception area, while you catch your breath. This room will do nicely to offer your esteemed guest a cup of tea." Katherine glanced around approvingly.

"You're a lifesaver, Katherine. You all are."

The morning mail had already arrived. Frances spotted a few envelopes in the pigeon-holes as she ran the duster over the top. She paused. Who did the sorting? What a pity the maid was laid low; she'd have been the best source of information, unless she only took care of the bedrooms. The servant hierarchy still confused Frances on occasion.

She paused to think again. Figuring out the sorting probably wouldn't have told them anything. Most members only dropped in once or twice a week or less, so mail sitting uncollected would be as unremarkable as an additional letter appearing between mail deliveries.

She finished with the reception area and headed towards the office.

It was sparsely, but adequately furnished, with two locked desk drawers and a filing cabinet. The only telephone was installed in a cabinet in the hallway, available for general use. It held a chair and a notepad and pen. Frances assumed it was meant to allow for taking notes during calls.

She gave the office furniture a good sweep. It wasn't exactly dusty, but the lack of staff made itself felt in a slight air of neglect. A couple of dead leaves from a potted plant on a side table and stained blotting paper showed that Dot was either too busy to look after these things herself or too used to having enough maids to take care of the tidying.

Frances picked up the leaves and replaced the blotting paper. She frowned as she noticed stains on the rug. Someone had stepped on it with wet soles and left a dirty imprint. The stain was too big to come from a ladies' heel, so she assumed Dot had worn galoshes and neglected to take them off in the cloak room.

"Frances?" Her mother-in-law knocked on the door.

"Coming."

Together, they swept the staircase and the upper hallway, before Dot called them down. She'd returned to a more cheerful frame of mind. "I'd appreciate it if you could join me. Her ladyship might have questions that I couldn't rightly answer, in my position. Otherwise, she'll simply have to take us as she finds us."

"I wish we could stick around," Poppy said. "Only we have an appointment with an old friend and she's not on the phone."

"We'll be fine without you," Dot said.

"I don't doubt it. You'll tell us all about it when we see you later. By the way, Katherine, we've invited all members of the Victory Circle for afternoon tea today."

Katherine mouthed to Frances, "That's Sarah."

The sisters were barely out of the door, when a limousine pulled up. A gentleman in an overcoat, heavy muffler and a soft bowler hat rang the doorbell before he helped a lady out of the car. A fur stole kept her warm.

Dot curtsied as she opened the door. "Your ladyship. And Mr. —"

"Mr. Bernardo is here as my man of affairs." The lady swept in, with a genial smile and a regal posture meant to set people at ease while intimidating them just a little. Aunt Mildred and Uncle Sal had arrived.

Frances watched from the lounge. Uncle Sal fussed with Aunt Mildred's coat. His manner straddled the line between subservient and capable. She inwardly applauded him.

Dot pointed him to the cloak room. "If your ladyship would follow me?"

Aunt Mildred beamed at her. "What a pleasant place this is. I congratulate you."

The manageress relaxed a little. "We've tried to keep everything as dear Lady Pemberton would've wished it."

"Most commendable." She waited for Uncle Sal to return from the cloak room before she moved on.

They entered the lounge. A bouquet of roses, procured in the greatest haste only a few minutes ago, cheered up the room. The fire guard needed black-leading, but the strategic placement of tables hid that fact.

Aunt Mildred allowed herself to be seated in the most comfortable chair. Uncle Sal chose a seat far enough to allow the women some privacy, yet close enough to listen to every word. Dot introduced Katherine and Frances, as a member of long standing and her daughter-in-law.

"Your ladyship." Frances curtsied.

"How delightful." Aunt Mildred peered through her pince-nez. "Do I detect a slight Australian accent, my dear?"

"My daughter-in-law and my son are visiting from Adelaide," Katherine said.

"Splendid." A benevolent smile accompanied the statement.

"Would you care for tea, my lady?" Frances asked.

"We have English Breakfast, Earl Grey, Lapsang Oolong, and Darjeeling," Dot said.

"How delightful. Darjeeling sounds lovely."

Frances headed towards the door.

"I'm afraid we're understaffed this week. It's this ghastly 'flu,'" Frances heard the manageress explain behind her back.

In the kitchen the tea tray had already been set with what she took to be the best china. She filled a teapot from the freshly boiled kettle.

"Wait." The cook, who was busy scrubbing carrots and turnips, nodded towards a biscuit barrel. "You'll have to go twice."

"I don't mind."

"Allow me." Uncle Sal, who'd followed her noiselessly, relieved her of the tray.

"Thank you, Mr. Bernardo."

She trotted after him. He'd obviously modelled parts of his role on Aunt Mildred's butler.

"You must forgive me for barging in on you at such short notice." Aunt Mildred selected a biscuit from the plate Frances had filled with the best the barrel had offered. "It was most fortuitous, really, remembering my dear friend Lady Pemberton, when I was racking my brain what to do with a recent legacy. It's so much nicer to give back to the world, isn't it, when we can? And what better way than to establish a club like this, which allows worthy women to be among themselves and to have a place where they can further their interests?"

"That's very enlightened," Dot said.

"It's sad but true that our struggles are far from over." Aunt Mildred stared at the portrait of their majesties on the wall. "The vote was only the beginning. If we want to achieve any kind of equality, it has to begin with friendship, and solidarity."

Dot smiled. "Indeed, my lady."

"It's so easy to forget the roles women like your members have played during the fight for suffrage, and during the Great War. What I've come here for today, is to find out exactly how the Athena Club operates and what I'd need to do to accomplish a similar feat." Aunt Mildred adjusted her pince-nez. "Mr. Bernardo will take notes of the financial particulars. But first, I have a question for you, Katherine. Is there anything you'd suggest as an improvement?"

Katherine was taken by surprise. That question hadn't been on their list. "I honestly couldn't say. I've never had any reason to complain."

"How about your daughter-in-law, as a newcomer?"

Francs pretended to mull over the question. "The only thing that comes to my mind is the reception area. I'd rather be kept waiting until I'm allowed in than have everybody be able to enter at all hours. Unless that's the London way?"

Did Dot glower at her?

"We're working on that. Like I mentioned, we're short-handed at the moment. Normally I'm either overlooking the reception or we use an automatic opener. It's been broken this past week," the manageress hurried to explain.

"What a very commendable system, one I hope you'll be able to fully implement again soon," Aunt Mildred said as she finished her tea.

Frances suppressed a small grin. Dot had just confirmed that the letter could have been delivered by anybody, walking in from the street.

"If you don't mind showing me around and answering a few questions?" Aunt Mildred held out her hand to Uncle Sal, so he could help her up.

Frances and Katherine took their leave. Now it was Aunt Mildred's star turn.

Katherine had decided to run a few errands while she waited for the Victory Circle meeting. In the meantime, Frances headed towards Oxford Street and Selfridge's, where Jack awaited her for lunch. They'd arranged to meet Uncle Sal and Aunt Mildred later. It wouldn't do to be seen together in the vicinity of the Athena Club.

The restaurant at the top floor never ceased to dazzle Frances, but today she also appreciated the convenient location, close to tube and bus stops. They'd finished their steak-and-kidney pies and were considering pudding, when a waiter approached them. "Are you Mr. Sullivan?"

"Yes?"

"There's a phone message for you." Only an arched eyebrow told Frances that such an occurrence wasn't a usual event.

The waiter slipped Jack a note and left them.

"What is it?" she asked as Jack read the note.

"There's been a development, at the club."

Chapter 11

To Frances's surprise, they took a cab to a Lyon's Corner House, a mere five-minute walk from the Athena.

Upstairs were secluded booths. In one of them sat Katherine, with a shivering Sarah by her side.

"I've had another letter." Sarah's hand shook as she fished it from her handbag.

"I want my money tonight. Leave it at 7pm in this envelope, underneath the alms box of St. George the Evangelist, in Red Lion Square. Come alone. Until death do us part, your loving husband."

Frances studied the typed envelope. Again, it was addressed to Sarah Blake.

"I've only got seven pounds." Sarah blinked back tears.

"It'll do," Jack said.

"What if it doesn't?"

"It will. He's not stupid. Look at the place he chose. Busy enough to hide, yet secluded enough so he can watch you."

"What am I supposed to do?" Sarah asked.

"Follow his instructions. And you'll add your own letter to the envelope. Demand a meeting, to discuss matters. Tell him otherwise there's no chance of you coming up with more money."

Frances took notepad and pen from her handbag.

"My hands are shaking so bad, I can hardly write," Sarah said.

"I'd do it for you, only he might notice if the handwriting's not yours," Frances said.

"What do I tell Harold? I never go out alone at night."

"Leave him a message, that you're staying out for dinner with the Victory Circle." Katherine squeezed Sarah's hand. "It's scary, but it'll soon be over."

Frances nodded, although she felt it in her bones that the blackmailer would never willingly stop.

Sending Sarah home alone to fetch the money and prepare for her ordeal pained Frances. Yet she agreed with Jack that the blackmailer likely watched her flat. George didn't fear his wife, but he might feel threatened if he caught on that she had support.

The only thing they could do was figure out how to keep watch on the alms box of St. George the Evangelist, or at least its close surroundings.

"I'll do it," Uncle Sal said as they discussed the situation at Aunt Mildred's. "An old, lame bloke like me is as good as invisible."

"You're not old, or lame," Frances protested. Her godfather limped only a little, unless cold, damp weather or undue exertion took their toll.

He twinkled at her. "Bless you, love. Give me my make-up bag and I'll give old Father Time a run for his money."

Tinkerbell protested. He'd snuggled up on Uncle Sal's lap while his mistress studied a sheaf of notes. She'd been in a state of quiet excitement ever since Jack and Frances had arrived. Leo took a nap. Chasing a ball with the older corgi had worn him out.

"We'll take the car out for a spin around Red Lion Square. There should be a pub where you can keep watch. In London, there's always a pub." She tapped her finger on the notes. "I wonder what else is going on."

"What do you mean?"

"There's something not quite right at the Athena. The sums don't add up."

"In what way?" Jack asked.

"Have a look. At the top is the yearly stipend the club receives from Lady Pemberton's estate. I had a chat with one of the board members, to prepare for my role."

"Which would have received two curtain calls at least at the Palladium." Uncle Sal kissed his fingertips. Tinkerbell woofed.

"Thank you. Anyway, you've seen for yourself how little staff there is and how sparse the amenities are. There should be daily newspapers and magazines. The lift is out of order, and no footman to carry up luggage, and to have only the man, one upstairs maid, two parlour maids and one help for cook is preposterous."

"She did say that the club was affected like everyone else," Frances said.

"It shouldn't. The stipend is a fixed sum, one that should be ample to keep up standards. Not long ago, the Athena had a dozen servants on the payroll." Aunt Mildred insisted.

Jack took the notes. Frances had no idea how many servants were deemed acceptable in London, but Jack might. And he'd be able to tally reasonable expenses to a shilling, as a business owner.

"What do you think? The manageress embezzles funds?"

"Either that, or she is also paying off a blackmailer. There should be at least another £200 per annum available for personnel. I wish I could get my hands on their account books and the guest books too."

The germ of an idea formed in Frances's head. It would have to wait though, if they wanted to take a geek around Red Lion Square.

Jack acted as chauffeur. He'd donned the smart uniform and cap that went with the job. Despite Aunt Mildred's leaving the driving in

London to her nephew or her butler, her late husband had used the services of a chauffeur. The uniform had been left over from those days.

Uncle Sal leant on a walking stick as he limped down the stairs. Heavy grooves ran from his nostrils to his mouth, and dark rings lined his eyes. What was visible of his hair under a soft cap was grey, thanks to a dose of talcum powder.

"Will that do?" He peered into the mirror and adjusted his shoulders to a slightly more hunched stance.

Frances inspected him. He'd put on an overcoat that had seen better days. The impression was now that of an elderly gent with a bit of money and pride left. Pickpockets wouldn't be interested in him as a mark, while he'd be right at home in a café, or a pub. Frances hoped for the first. Eateries tended to have clean windows and brighter lights better suited to watching than ale houses.

While Jack fetched Aunt Mildred's limousine, a cape and muffler hid Uncle Sal's disguise. They didn't want tongues wagging any more than they already did about the strange folks at the Clifton mansion.

Aunt Mildred and Uncle Sal took the back seat. Jack studied the road map one more time before they set off. For Frances, London was a maze, full of surprises at every turn. But today, getting lost was not an option.

They'd timed their arrival with the exodus of clerks and typists from the offices in Holborn. In summer, the public garden in the square would have been a pleasant spot for observation. Frances decided to come back during the day.

"There's a tea-room that's still open," Jack pointed out. "If our pigeon uses the underground, he'll pass by the windows on the way between the church and Holborn Station. It's the same way Sarah will come by, so you have a chance to observe if he follows her." Unspoken was the fear that George might be lying in wait for the woman. If his anger outweighed his greed, she was in grave danger – literally.

Uncle Sal left the cape on the backseat before he stepped out. Jack knew better than to assist him. In his chauffeur's uniform he would only have drawn attention to Uncle Sal.

"And now?" he asked.

"Now we go home and wait," Frances reluctantly said.

Leo and Tinkerbell shared a dog treat between them. They'd have to do with Aunt Mildred's manicured back garden for their final outing of the day. Until the phone rang to say that Uncle Sal's vigil was over, and Sarah was safe, they'd all stay close by.

Meanwhile, Uncle Sal nursed a cup of coffee while he waited for an omelet. The tea-room did a brisk business with shop assistants too tired to cook for themselves or living in a lodging house with only a gas ring in their room.

A couple of housewives with bulging shopping bags chatted about their neighbours (no better than they should be), husbands with a tendency to expect a Sunday roast without loosening the purse strings (they were all the same), and the lack of morals since the war (shocking).

If the waitress decided it was those two women who caused Uncle Sal to divert his attention to the window, so much the better.

Sarah should be arriving any minute now. He wished he'd ordered soup. Waiting for soup to cool off was a natural thing, whereas an omelet needed instant eating.

"There you are." The waitress sat down his plate. He counted his coins. If he saw Sarah and someone hard on her heels, he'd have no time to lose. Placing the money for his bill on the saucer now relieved his conscience.

He risked a quick glance at the wall clock. Ten minutes to seven. Sarah wouldn't dare be too early. He tucked into his meal, all the while glancing outside from under half-lowered lids.

There. His heart beat faster. A woman in a grey coat and a red cloche went towards the church. This morning, Frances had worn the cloche, purchased in Paris and not likely to be seen twice in Holborn. She'd given it to Sarah to make her stand out in the crowd.

Uncle Sal counted under his breath. Sixty seconds had passed, and still he hadn't spotted a pursuer. Now he'd see if it stayed like this on Sarah's way back to the underground.

Chapter 12

"You're fast becoming a permanent fixture," Dot greeted Katherine and Frances. Was her smile forced? If she was fiddling with the accounts, Aunt Mildred's visit must have rattled her, Frances thought.

Katherine chuckled. "Isn't it lucky that Poppy and Dash arrived in town during a week when I have so many free days for once? And of course, darling Frances loves the opportunity to hear our stories about the war and our fight for the vote."

"It's like being part of it," Frances said. She fought the urge to scan the pigeon-holes.

"Count yourself lucky you weren't there," Dot said. "After all is said and done, there were too many sacrifices made during the war." Her jaw tightened.

Frances wished she knew more about the woman.

"But that's neither here nor there. You'll find the sisters in the reading room." Dot picked up a parcel from the reception desk and winced. "Ouch." Blood dripped onto the wooden surface.

"Let me have a look." Frances took Dot's hand. "It's a cut, but a nasty one." She wound her handkerchief around the injured fingers.

"First aid materials are in the kitchen," Dot said.

"I'll have you fixed up in a jiffy," Katherine said. "Come with me."

Frances's conscience pinged. She hoped the cut wasn't too bad. She ripped the bloody brown paper of the parcel, thus revealing a biscuit tin from Fortnum's, courtesy of Aunt Mildred, and in one fell swoop disposing of the means by which they'd engineered the incident.

When Dot returned with Katherine, her right hand sported a thick bandage covering two fingers.

"I've told Dot to rest the hand for at least two days," Katherine said. "I've seen wounds turn septic because of undue exertion." She winked at Frances, to confirm that this was a little white lie.

Dot groaned. "I can't just do nothing. The paperwork's already piled up as it is."

"I can do it for you. I've done a course," Frances said.

"It's too much to ask," Dot said regretfully.

"Nonsense, it'll do me good to feel useful after being spoilt rotten for ages."

"If you're sure? The most urgent things are the letters. Otherwise it's only typing up the menus and a few other bits."

Frances hoped Dot would leave her alone in the office for a while, so she could snoop around. In her purse she carried all the equipment she needed to pick the drawer locks where she expected to find the account books.

Her mother in-law saw to it. She called Dot away, to discuss a charity event needing her support. "The venue's not far from here, and it would be so good to have your opinion on arrangements." That should give Frances sufficient time to sleuth, before Dot returned to help her with the letters.

She typed up the menus in a hurry, grateful her fingers hadn't lost their nimbleness, and then she typed a message to herself, to have a sample of the machine. After working the busiest telephone switchboard in Adelaide, the Underwood typewriter posed no difficulty.

Neither did the locks. Uncle Sal had taught her his tricks from his Vaudeville days, and she was well equipped to pick much more difficult locks than these ones. Why, a hairpin would have done the job.

The accounts were another matter. Try as she might, she couldn't make head nor tail of the entries. Large sums were listed as expenses in 1929, and 1930, and then they stopped. With her blood pulsing loudly in her ears, she copied the information. She daren't risk borrowing the books.

Her gaze travelled to the filing cabinet. Could she risk snooping in there?

She returned the accounts, locked the drawer and peeked out of the door. From afar came the murmur of a conversation. Two sets of footsteps made her withdraw.

Her notes would have to do for now.

She tapped the corners of the typed menus on the desk, to align them neatly. Back went the cover over the typewriter. Reluctantly, she left the room, only to run into Sarah whose face was drained of all colour.

"He was here," Sarah whispered. For an instant, she let Frances glimpse another envelope. "I'll meet you as arranged."

Despite her paleness, Sarah showed surprising resilience, Frances thought. After last night's fears, now she strolled calmly to the tea-room where they'd first met and waited for Frances to arrive. Katherine had stayed at the club, to worm a little more information out of the sisters.

Hot, strong coffee fortified both women. After the first few sips, Sarah handed Frances the letter. The envelope contained a single note. "British Museum, 4pm. I'll be wearing a plaid cape and a brown cap. Another £5 needed to open discussions. Until death do us part."

"He agreed." Sarah seemed almost shocked. In her note to George, she'd demanded a public area, during the afternoon for a meeting. "Maybe he'll see reason and leave me alone." She opened a jewellery box containing a pretty set of ruby earrings and a square cut diamond ring. "These were my mum's. They're worth much more than £5." A tear ran down her cheek. "They're all I've got left of her."

"You can't hand them over. They're too precious." Anger rose in Frances.

"I have no choice. I'll do whatever it takes. You see, Harold and I always wanted a family. I won't have George destroy my child's life." Her hand wandered to her belly.

"You're having a baby?"

"The doctor confirmed it this morning." Sarah put away the jewellery box. "Mum would have understood."

That settled it for Frances. They would find George and end his vile machinations, before Sarah endured any more.

A weak late afternoon sun shone on the British Museum. Frances had dressed in the blonde wig she used during her rare stage appearances as "Signorina Francesca", assistant to "Salvatore the Magnificent". A new hat and a coat borrowed from Aunt Mildred made her unrecognisable as she admired the shop windows within a stone's throw of the museum.

A milliner attracted her attention. Its polished plate glass and mirrors inside the main room reflected the people walking by. She'd be hard-pressed to miss a man with such conspicuous garments as George had described.

Uncle Sal was engrossed in his newspaper. The wooden bench he'd chosen also allowed him a good look at the museum entrance and towards the exit of the underground station. Only an eagle-eyed observer would notice the holes poked into The Times.

Aunt Mildred had opted to keep to her usual appearance. A well-kept mature gentlewoman blended right in with a multitude of others. She fixed her pince-nez as she admired the exhibits in the entrance of the museum, thus keeping an eye on Sarah who lingered outside.

Jack ambled between underground station and bus stop. He carried a bouquet of flowers and showed all the signs of a man waiting for his girlfriend to arrive.

He was the first to spot the arrival of a man in a plaid cape and brown cap. From afar, Sarah also saw him. She froze to the spot.

The man pushed towards the busy street. Then, he was gone, and Jack heard a dull thud and the squeaking of brakes. A woman screamed, "He's dead."

Sarah ran towards them, until Uncle Sal blocked her way.

Jack's mind reeled as he watched the scene on the street, where George's body lay bloodied and lifeless.

The driver of a Humber sat behind the wheel. The door was open, ready for him to step out. "He fell in front of me, I swear to it." He repeated this over and over, until a pair of bobbies approached him.

Jack slipped away. There was nothing he could do - for now.

Because he was certain the driver told the truth.

George had fallen directly in front of the car. He'd also had help.

Jack had seen a gloved hand pushing him.

Chapter 13

"Murder? But why?" Frances asked. She'd taken the shocked Sarah home in a taxi and tucked her in with a hot water bottle. Only after the woman had calmed down, did she frugally return to Aunt Mildred's by bus.

"That's a good question. I hope Sir Reginald will help us shed light on it," Jack said.

"He'll be here within the hour." Aunt Mildred held out a treat for both Tink and Leo, who happily followed the older dog like a shadow. She swore they both knew they were blood relatives.

"I hope we've done the right thing, not telling the police what you saw." Uncle Sal rubbed his ankle. He'd had to move fast to block Sarah, too fast for his old injuries.

"I can still come forward," Jack said. "The important thing is that the police don't connect Sarah to the dead man. Once it's official, there's no protecting her from the outfall."

"At least she can't be blamed for George's death," Frances said.

"Can you be so certain?" Sir Reginald Fitzpatrick asked after listening to their story. He'd arrived in a commendable hurry.

"You must be joking. Sarah was within our sight the whole time." Aunt Mildred glowered daggers at her old friend.

"She could have had an accomplice. What about her second husband? He had as much of a motive as she did, to get rid of the man," Sir Reginald pointed out.

"That'll be easy to prove. He was at his place of work." Frances gave him the address. She'd asked Sarah if she should ring him up, in case she needed his support. Sarah had declined but mentioned the name of the employer.

She asked, "Is there any way you could find out if George's body has been identified yet? If he had Sarah's letter on him when he died, it might still lead back to her."

"You're absolutely convinced she had no idea her first husband was still alive, until she received the letter?"

"Absolutely. I'd put my hand in the fire for it. Why was she supposed to doubt it, with George declared missing and later, dead?" Aunt Mildred thumped the table. The corgis stared at her, round-eyed, before they snarled at Sir Reginald.

His lips twitched. "I've heard less impassioned speeches in the House of Commons. I didn't say you weren't right. There must be thousands of widows in the same position, but also thousands who jumped at the chance of leaving behind one unsatisfactory husband and choosing to wed again despite evidence that the first spouse was still alive."

"Well, Sarah didn't know, even if it appears odd that George waited so long to resurface," Frances said. She felt like thumping the table herself, if only good manners had allowed it.

"I can think of a reason," Sir Reginald said. "What if he used the battlefields to slip away?" His train of thoughts ran along the same lines as theirs, Frances noticed. With any luck, he'd also follow their further deductions.

Aunt Mildred frowned. "Desert? But there's never been an amnesty for deserters, even if they are no longer shot at dawn. Desertion is still a crime."

"It is, yet the government prefers to ignore it. There's been enough bad blood over court-martialling and imprisoning veterans. People have more than enough to worry about without reminding them of those terrible years," Sir Reginald said.

They all turned towards Jack, the only veteran in the room. Sir Reginald had served in the war ministry, but Jack had been in the thick of it, after enlisting in Australia with his mates as soon as the fighting began. "It's not exactly easy to forget when you've got old soldiers starving in the streets. But that's neither here nor there. Poverty still doesn't excuse blackmail."

"I'll see what I can do," Sir Reginald said. He drummed his fingertips on the table, alerting Tinkerbell and Leo again. "What I don't comprehend is, if you want to keep a low profile, why chose an attire that is impossible to overlook? And why select a crowded area?"

"We suggested a busy place, to protect Sarah," Frances said.

"She selected the British Museum?"

"Not specifically, but something along the lines."

"Then why didn't this George fella name a park or a café to meet her at? There are enough quiet places in London where she'd still have been safe. He ran an awful risk of running into someone who knew him from ages ago."

"Unless he'd changed a lot. Scars can do that," Jack said.

"I don't know. I feel as if we're missing something," Sir Reginald said.

Frances had to admit she agreed with him, although she couldn't explain why.

"Him dying doesn't add up," Jack said. "Unless he's had the misfortune to run into a mortal enemy on his way to meet Sarah, which is highly improbable."

"A falling out with an accomplice? Maybe the joker who delivered the blackmail notes," Uncle Sal suggested.

"Unlikely. It would have made more sense to wait until George had collected the money and then rob him."

"Unless his conscience got in the way." Frances surprised herself. "What if the idea of seeing Sarah face to face made him reconsider? If he told his partner in crime he'd stop or even return the extorted money, it wouldn't have gone down well."

"And the partner who was watching the same way we did, decided he'd rather bump off good old George before he'd feel the long arm of the law for extortion." Jack pressed a kiss on her forehead. "I think you've nailed it on the head."

Sir Reginald smiled at them. "You still have some of the best minds I've seen in the business. All right. I'll look into the report on the death and see what I can do. In the meantime, let's raise our glasses in a toast. Whatever happened to George, your friend's woes are over."

Chapter 14

"It's only beginning." Katherine toyed with her kedgeree. She'd already retired when Jack and Frances had returned home, for once dog-less. Leo and Tink had been curled up together so happily they couldn't bring themselves to wake the puppy.

Since Aunt Mildred's maid and the butler both doted on the corgis, he'd be well looked after, without causing too much trouble for his hostess.

"What do you mean? George is dead." Frances shivered at the thought. Not that he deserved her pity, but it was a gruesome end, and then there was the poor man who'd driven the Humber. He wouldn't be able to shake it off that easily, either.

"That's true, but if he really wasn't working alone, his accomplice could pick up where he left off. I'm almost sure Sarah wasn't the only target," Katherine said.

Jack stared at this mum. "What makes you think so?"

"After Frances left, a few other members arrived. Two of them had post waiting for them. I'm not one hundred percent certain of the meaning, but I noticed one of the letters had no stamp or postmark."

"And the recipient?" Frances put down her toast. She'd lost her appetite.

"A war widow, or rather she was widowed twice and only recently remarried."

"A bit like Sarah," Jack said.

"Yes. In which case his partner could carry on. Who knows how many women they've spied on once George had located Sarah?"

"We've got to tell Sir Reginald," Frances said.

"What's he supposed to do, unless we have a clear suspect? One who isn't in the morgue." Jack clasped her hand.

***

The phone rang, giving Katherine a start. It had only recently been installed in the drawing room, as a present from Jack.

"Yes?" Frances heard her say. "I see. . . Right away."

A familiar click told Frances the receiver had been returned to the cradle.

"It was a message from Lady Mildred," Katherine said.

When they'd first met during their sea voyage from Adelaide to London, she'd been the Honourable Mrs Walter Clifton, but a death in the family had changed her title. Frances still had trouble figuring out the correct addresses for first, second, and lesser sons of noble houses. She stuck to one rule. If a title was inherited, the first name would be used, as in Lady Mildred. Had the title been acquired through marriage, it would have been Lady Clifton.

Katherine let Jack finish his final bite of sausage, before she continued. "She asks you to visit with her as soon as possible. There's been a development."

"I'll fetch our coats," Frances said.

"Shall we take a cab?" Jack asked.

She peered out of the window. There were no rain clouds in sight, and the bus stop was only a few minutes away. "Let's stick to public transport."

"Frugal as always." Jack grinned at her.

"There's no need to waste your money."

Aunt Mildred already had another visitor. Sir Reginald stood in the back garden, watching Tinkerbell and Leo play tug-of-war with a knotted string.

Frances's step faltered. His presence did not bode well. Neither did his grim expression.

"What have you gotten yourselves into?" he asked without so much as a hello.

She exchanged a worried look with Jack.

"What's so bad? Shielding an innocent woman's reputation wouldn't bother you enough to leave your office," Jack said.

"I've looked into the report," Sir Reginald said. He didn't mention what pretext he'd used, and they didn't pry. "To cut a long story short, the dead man still had his appendix. If your friend told you the truth, about his operation, the man in the morgue isn't George Blake."

"That doesn't make sense. He fit the description, and he was in the right place at the right time for their appointment." Frances's confusion grew.

"That's not the only strange thing. The doctor who examined the body had a second, closer look. Whoever the man was, he'd have died anyway. There was a stab wound in his back, and traces of poison in the blood."

"So, there's no doubt he was murdered."

Jack steadied Frances. "We suspected that much. After all, I did spot a hand pushing the poor joker onto the road."

"But poison and a stab wound prove the killer was prepared, whereas a shove sounds more like a spur of the moment thing. Did the victim have anything on him that helps with the identification? Maybe he's got a family waiting for him at home." Frances marvelled at her newfound calm. A year ago, the closest she'd come to dealing with crime were petty thefts. Now, dead bodies and solving murder cases were part of her life, and that of Jack, Uncle Sal, and Aunt Mildred.

Sir Reginald shrugged. "The report says he was malnourished, with frostbite, and shrapnel scars. He'd been a veteran but that's all his body told us. The cape and hat were old and probably came from a charitable organisation."

"A veteran," Jack said. "That has to be the connection."

Sir Reginald consulted his watch. "I'll have to toddle off. We'll keep in touch."

They ventured indoors, with the exhausted dogs by their side.

Aunt Mildred had already heard the story, because she came straight to the point. "Where do we go from here?"

"I don't know that we can do anything," Frances said. "We're no closer to finding George than we were yesterday."

Aunt Mildred snorted. "We won't give up. That poor woman has been through enough to have this constant threat hanging over her head. How is she coping?"

"She was shaky when I left her, but hopeful that she'd never hear another word from that brute." Frances shivered, despite the warmth from the fireplace. "We have to tell her it was the wrong body."

Chapter 18

Frances took Leo along as she went to meet her husband. The puppy still shied away from the noisy London traffic and stayed glued to her side until they'd reached the square. The city was full of more or less hidden gardens, some private, most open to the public.

She'd left her mother-in-law to fuss over Sarah and to distract her with insights about motherhood. Were they doing the right thing, letting the poor woman believe her tormentor was dead? Or should they come clean?

Leo yapped, as if he'd read her mind. "Too right," she told him. "This isn't the moment to add fuel to the fire."

"What isn't?" Jack greeted her. He'd spent the day listening to a number of veterans. They were easy to spot, hawking cheap wares or lining up outside soup kitchens.

Leo rubbed his head on Jack's leg. "I haven't forgotten." He flung a ball, not far because the puppy could become overexcited. The last thing they needed was to disturb a courting couple on the other end of the square.

Frances rubbed her gloved hands together. How people ever got used to the damp chill in the air was beyond her. She peered at her husband. "Have you been waiting long? We had a bit more of an upset than expected."

"Not to worry. As long as we're making progress."

"I hope we do."

Leo dropped the ball at Jack's feet. His stubby tail wagged as fast as it could.

"Here you go again, mate." He turned to Frances. "What I've been thinking about is the letters, or rather the typewriter. You don't stumble upon a machine that easily. And I remember it taking more than a few tries to hit the keys properly, when I tried my hand at typing."

"Too right they can be hard to handle." Frances grinned at her husband. "I think you're on the right track because I noticed something."

"Splendid." He planted a kiss on the top of her nose. "What is it?"

"I'll show you, once Leo's ready to leave." She crossed her fingers. Please, don't let me be wrong, she thought. This is our only real clue.

Back home, she handed Jack the magnifying glass his mother used for close needlework. "Exhibits one and two." They'd held on to the letters to Sarah, for safekeeping. She hadn't dared take them with her.

"What am I looking at?" Jack asked.

"The capital B. I only saw it today, when Sarah handed over the new message. There's a tiny bit missing in the lower part."

Jack scanned the envelopes.

The flaw was small and easy to overlook. "I'm not imagining things, am I?" Frances scrutinised the words again.

"You're not."

"It's also there, in the letters. It proves the men were working together. All these messages were written on the same typewriter. It's not the one in the Athena. I've compared it with the sample I kept."

"You thought the manageress was behind it, with or without the man's assistance?"

"It would have been the most obvious possibility. You must have thought so, too."

He confirmed it with a shrug.

"I assume we both wanted to be sure, to spare your mum unnecessary worry."

"True. Anyway, thanks to your discovery we're a lot closer to solving this case. If we find where, we find who." A wide grin spread over Jack's face. "You're the smartest girl I've ever met."

"Why, thank you, sir. You're not too bad either." Frances leant closer to her husband, only to be startled by the arrival of his mother.

"What are you doing?"

Frances pointed out the flawed envelopes. "Did you notice if there was a chipped B on the letter Emily received?"

"I'll see what I can find out. Excellent detective work, Frances."

"How did Sarah take the news about George being alive?" Jack asked.

"We haven't told her yet. The doctor ordered rest and peace of mind, for the baby's sake." Worry lines appeared on Katherine's forehead.

"Just be certain not to leave her out of your sight when she goes to the club."

"She'll stay at home until I tell her otherwise. Why?" Katherine asked.

"We still haven't the foggiest why the poor chap was killed. It could have been George who bumped him off. In that case, who can say what he'll do to Sarah?" Jack wondered.

"But the new letter came from a different person," Katherine said.

"Unless it's what he wants us to think. I wouldn't put it past him to taunt Sarah in this twisted way. I think he's after as much money as he can wring out of her, but he also enjoys inflicting pain."

"There's another possibility," Frances said. "If George had an idea his partner was about to double-cross him, he could have chosen those horrid clothes as a kind of disguise. He only needed to show his instructions to Sarah to his mate, and then offer some poor man a few coins to put on the cape and the hat."

"You think, the second man then attacked him from behind, in the mistaken belief it was George, and he could take over the racket?"

"Wouldn't he have noticed afterwards he got the wrong man?" Katherine asked.

"Not likely, with those injuries. I'll spare you the details."

"If this theory is correct, we have two dangerous men out there, and Sarah is caught in the middle," Frances said.

"Emily as well. We mustn't forget her," Katherine said.

"We won't. At least now we have something concrete to go on." Jack tapped on the envelopes.

Frances sighed. "If we succeed in finding the correct typewriter. Only, where do we start?"

***

At Aunt Mildred's, Frances slung a hand knitted scarf around Uncle Sal's neck. Large holes in it as well as the pattern of yellow and green stripes explained why the item had ended up at a jumble sale at Aunt Mildred's church.

She'd graciously purchased a whole suitcase full of donated clothes, which she intended to donate again. In the meantime, they'd come in useful as disguise.

A wide-brimmed felt hat and a pea-coat with a ragged hem completed Uncle Sal's outfit.

"I wish I could go with you," Aunt Mildred said.

"I'm sure there'll be another opportunity," Frances said, although she shared the sentiment. The undercover roles were always the most exciting to play.

Uncle Sal picked up his list. "Wish me luck."

"You'll be bonzer," Frances assured him as she adjusted his hat.

He set off, with only an hour to do his sleuthing before the typing bureaus closed for the day.

Jack was out on a similar mission. They'd decided it was unlikely that George would have frequented a business in the affluent parts of the city. With his sort of material to type, they were looking for a place where he could rent a machine for his private use, probably in a back room. There couldn't be many typing bureaus that fit their bill.

Because George used to work on the docks, Uncle Sal was heading towards the river and the East End. The list in his pocket was the result of their joint efforts, using the telephone directory.

While Aunt Mildred had rung up companies, to enquire if customers could use one of the machines, Frances had written down the addresses of those who said yes.

Aunt Mildred had enjoyed herself. She'd prudently modelled her speech on her maid's. No real lady would undertake this sort of task herself.

Uncle Sal was on his way to discover as much as possible from the enterprises in question.

Since not every small firm had a telephone installed, Jack's task was searching for office plaques and other signs. Uncle Sal had been so chipper at the idea of donning a disguise and setting out, Frances hadn't had the heart to admit to him that she thought it most likely George had used a one-person bureau, operating from a single room.

"We can consider ourselves lucky that he won't want to show himself openly, since his whole scheme depends on being invisible.

Otherwise, he could have joined a club," Aunt Mildred said, switching back from dropping the h's to her clipped vowels. Watching Uncle Sal rehearse had taught her a lot.

"Like the Athena?" Frances asked.

"Yes, only that's out of the question if he's playing dead," Aunt Mildred said. "We can but hope the men discover something."

One of the problems Jack had, was the vast variety in fortunes. Too often only one street separated the well-to-do from those barely scraping by in the metropolis. He'd decided to begin his search around Holborn and Bloomsbury, where St. George the Evangelist and the British Museum were located. If their bird had selected these areas for conducting his vile business, he needed intimate knowledge of the neighbourhood.

Bloomsbury was mostly home to the bohemian set, while Holborn attracted lawyers, barristers, and businessmen who hadn't quite reached their pinnacle yet.

He betted on the fact that authors and men of the law relying on long written briefs would be in need of the occasional typist. The smaller the business, the likelier it was that George had been able to hire a machine.

At least they knew one of the dates he'd been in. His response to Katherine's demand had been almost instant. That narrowed it down to the evening and early morning.

With dogged determination he trudged on, street after street, and alley after alley. At least every third typist he asked would have been only too happy to rent out her machine for an hour or two, yet none of them had done so lately.

Most of them were young women, who'd struck out on their own to support their families. He took care to leave them a sixpence, for their time.

He nearly gave up for the day, when he knocked on a shabby but well-scrubbed door, with black lettering on plate glass announcing yet another typist's bureau.

A woman in a business suit greeted him. Behind a partition, a typewriter fairly rattled along.

"How can I be of assistance, sir?" the woman enquired.

"Do you only take on typing jobs you tackle yourself? Or is it possible to do one's own writing, if it's something frightfully confidential?"

She raised her eyebrows at him. "I assure you that silence is part of our stock in trade."

Behind her, he noticed a photograph of an older sergeant and a young recruit. The young man looked vaguely familiar. He changed his prepared speech and improvised. "Gosh, yes, rather. The thing is, I'm looking for a long-lost war mate, and I've been told he was trying to, you know, flog some rather hot and not altogether very true memoirs. Probably nothing in it, but Major ... well, the name's of no consequence, long story short is, I was asked to locate the fellow."

"A soldier?"

Jack nodded.

She knocked on the partition. "Would you please join us for a moment, Paul?"

A man in Jack's age came into view. His straw-coloured hair stuck up like a cock's comb. "I'm almost done, cousin. Some of these scientific words are the deuce to spell."

"It's not that. This gentleman has a question. Please, go ahead, Mr. —"

"Sullivan. Jack Sullivan, at your service."

Paul gaped at him. Recognition dawned in his eyes. "Captain Jack?"

"Sergeant Goode? How long's it been?"

"Summer of 1918. Last leave I had before the armistice."

They shook hands with genuine enthusiasm. "Now, what do you want to ask?" Paul asked.

Jack repeated his tale.

Paul shook his head. "Whoever this soldier is, he wasn't here. Hot stuff like that, he wouldn't dare knock on the door of any decent business. Too risky, that someone would accidentally glimpse a few words. Also, you must be pretty nimble and well-trained not to make a mess out of your typing, and wastepaper is not that easy to hide in a shared room. It's unlikely he'd have hired a machine." Disdain crept into his tone.

"What would you have done in his stead?"

"Have you tried the veterans' hangouts?"

"Only one pub so far."

The church bells struck six.

"Why don't you show your friend here?" the woman asked. "You can finish the job tomorrow."

"If you don't mind?" Jack asked both.

"I'm glad to be of service. My father served in the Boer War and in the Great War. If anyone can be prevented from spreading lies about our brave men, cousin Paul and I won't stand idly by," the woman declared.

Chapter 15

The running of the kitchen taps and thundering footsteps alerted Sarah to the arrival of the charwoman. Strictly speaking theirs wasn't a serviced flat, but once a week the rough work was taken care of.

Harold must have let the charwoman in, on his way to work. She dragged herself into a half upright position.

On her nightstand sat an empty cup. Harold had brought her morning tea and a plate with toast when she struggled to get out of bed.

Tears welled up. He was so good to her, so kind and gentle. He hadn't probed when he found her already in bed the night before. Instead, he'd heated soup and brought her a bowl. She'd explained her unaccustomed state with a migraine. The news about the baby would have to wait until she'd recovered. Otherwise, Harold would be worried sick.

The charwoman tapped on her bedroom door. "Shall I make you a nice cup of tea?"

"Yes, please." Sarah rubbed her forehead. Why did she feel so numb inside? She should be happy, elated even, or feel grief for George. Although he'd made her miserable soon enough, for a few, blissful weeks she'd been happy with him.

A cup was set next to her. "The master's said as I was to nip out for the doctor if you're no better."

"There's no need, really." Sarah forced herself to smile.

"Are you sure? It's no trouble. My sister's eldest is in service with the doctor, so she could put in a good word, that it's urgent-like."

"Quite sure, thank you."

"Is it the 'flu?" The woman took a step back. "Or that nasty foreign food them next door force on unsuspecting people?"

Sarah took "them next door" to be a retired civil servant and his wife who'd spent most of his career in India. They'd brought with them a manservant and a fondness for curries, which they freely shared. Since they had no need for a char, the woman looked upon them with suspicion.

"Only a headache. A good rest is all I need." To Sarah's relief, the woman took the hint and tiptoed out of the room.

She awoke in the afternoon, much recovered and ready to face the world. If she popped out now to visit Katherine and Frances, to thank them, she should be back before Harold came home. She searched in her purse for three pence, to ring them up from the public phone box and announce her visit. When the operator couldn't get a response, Sarah decided to stop at the butcher's for a chicken to roast, and to return home. Tonight, she'd tell Harold about the baby.

At the Athena Club, things were quiet. With Dot's hand still bandaged, Frances sorted through the morning mail and the letters from last night. Invoices, she set aside for the manageress to go through, but there were a few letters from members asking for accommodation in the next couple of months.

Like before, she read them out to Dot, who held the club's appointment book on her lap. While she turned the pages with her left hand, she checked the availability of the guest rooms and gave Frances instructions what to type.

The Athena appeared to be much sought after, with its members as far flung as Penzance and Fife.

"Most of our ladies were brought together by the war," Dot explained when Frances mentioned this. "They travelled from all over the country to train in London as nurses and work in the hospitals. Some went on to drive ambulances or they took over office posts, until the men came back home. If they came back." Her face clouded over.

Frances decided not to pry further. "There are three ladies we can't put up during their requested dates," she said after sifting through her notes."

"Can you give me the names again? Have they mentioned the reasons for their journey?"

Frances told her the names. "One is invited to a reunion, and the other two want to visit the summer exhibition at the Royal Academy."

"A reunion. Let's see who we can move around to make that happen. The other two ladies won't mind coming down at a later date, as long as they're together. Joined at the hip, those two are."

"What a marvellous memory you have," Frances praised her.

"It helps with the job. This isn't like a hotel, where customers come and go. We're more like an extended family."

"Do you keep notes? Do you think I should do that once we're back home, to help my husband with his business?"

"It can't hurt if he deals with repeat customers. Only I'd use discretion. Notes for yourself are fine, but you wouldn't want anyone to know their little foibles."

Frances agreed. "Too right that wouldn't be good. Do you think things like birthdays or wedding anniversaries, or maiden names could be useful?"

"Absolutely. Now, if you'd type up the answers, I'll tally up the invoices. Our suppliers are all honest people, but errors do happen."

Dot moved her lips as she silently did her sums.

Frances started typing.

Meanwhile, Katherine tried to broach the subject of the suspicious looking letter with the recipient. She could hardly ask Emily Pennington if she was being blackmailed. The bookcase in the library gave her an idea. They were both alone. Emily distractedly read an old issue of Good Housekeeping magazine. Or rather, Katherine thought, Emily pretended to read. She hadn't turned the pages for at least ten minutes.

"There it is." With a small cry of triumph, Katherine pulled Agatha Christie's "The Murder of Roger Ackroyd" from its shelf. "Have you read it?"

"Pardon?" Emily glanced up from the magazine.

"Sorry, I didn't mean to interrupt you. Have you read this mystery? I've been told it's the most ingenious novel. It starts with blackmail."

Emily's face drained of colour. "I don't read crime novels. They're—" She faltered.

"Too close for comfort?" Katherine strode to the door and closed it properly. "You'll have to forgive me, but if someone is threatening you, I might help. You see, you're not the only one." Please, let me be right, she thought.

"What are you saying?" Emily's body went rigid.

"I believe you found a letter in your pigeon-hole yesterday, one that distressed you. You're waiting for another missive, if I'm correct."

Emily's voice dropped to a panicked whisper. "How can you possibly know that? Unless you're in on this."

"I'm not, I promise. Like I said, you're not the only one. Would you care to tell me, in private?" Katherine considered fetching Frances. No,

Emily might clam up if faced with yet another person. "I'll have you back here at the club within the hour. I promise."

Emily answered her with a tiny nod.

On their way out, Katherine peeked into the office. "I'll pick you up later, Frances." Seeing Dot's curious expression, she added, "I've enlisted help with my errands, so you don't have to hurry."

Emily's story, told in starts and stops over coffee and scones in a secluded corner of an otherwise noisy tea-room, sounded painfully familiar.

Like with Sarah, Emily's husband hadn't returned from the war. "Missing, presumed dead, that's what the letter from the War Ministry said, in 1915. Even after he was declared dead, I waited another two years for more news, before I remarried, only to have my Carl be killed just before the armistice." Five years ago, Emily had become a wife again. "Carl's old chaplain was in charge of the ceremony. He never said a single word that I shouldn't marry again." A dry sob escaped her.

"What happened?"

"He wrote to me. He says I should've waited. He can have me up before the law, he says. And he will, if I don't pay him."

"Your first husband?"

"Yes. Alf never used to be this cruel when we were married, not even when he was in his cups, which was more often the case than not." Her face crumpled.

"Are you certain it's him?"

"Who else could it be? He called me Milly in the letter. Nobody else used that nickname, except for Alf."

How could that be? Katherine found it hard to believe that two ne'er-do-well husbands, missing on the battlefields, had returned to extort money from their wives at the same time, in the same place.

"Tell me everything you remember about Alf," Katherine said. "Don't be afraid. The law can't hurt you."

Chapter 16

"Two victims, same method of blackmail, same threat. The men have to be in cahoots," Jack said.

"I agree." Aunt Mildred, whose home had become the unofficial headquarters of their investigation, polished her pince-nez with unnecessary vigour. "To think that dear Lady Pemberton's legacy is reduced to being the unwitting means of extorting money from the very women she sought to support is unbearable."

"If it is the club," Frances interrupted.

"I'd love to exonerate the Athena, yet it's the link between the women," Aunt Mildred said.

"It's one link. What if it's the men? They could easily have met in the war."

Jack pulled out the notes his mother had given him. "We know where Alf did his initial training and in what regiment he served. If Sarah can pinpoint George's war history, we might be getting somewhere."

"There's also the possibility they crossed paths in a hospital, if George and Alf were injured in the war."

"Which is highly likely. I only had my wing clipped, but most of my mates had it worse, with the gas and the shelling." Jack rarely mentioned the wound he'd sustained in the last weeks of the war, but underneath his casual tone, Frances sensed the pain.

"That still wouldn't explain how the men happened to track down two women who'd changed surnames in a metropolis like London," Aunt Mildred said.

"And our birds would only have to say they were in touch with their wives, and there's no way to disprove that kind of statement. What a damnable situation."

"If we can figure out why they disappeared for all these years, Sir Reginald can scare them into shutting up. After all, the women have the death certificates to prove they had no idea the men survived." Frances remembered the sheer panic in Sarah's eyes, and the relief when she thought George was dead. She dreaded telling the woman the truth, that her tormentor was still out there.

"Death certificates. Of course!" Aunt Mildred exclaimed so loudly, Tink came running. She picked him up and cuddled him. "All births, deaths, marriages, and wills in the country are kept on file at Somerset House. It only costs a small fee to see them."

"So, George and Alf could have just gone there to find out if their wives remarried and their new married names?" Uncle Sal asked. He'd been uncharacteristically quiet.

Frances spotted a bundle of papers on his lap that he seemed to peruse on the sly. Had he been offered a new part in a motion picture? She wouldn't put it past him to decline, in case they needed him. He shouldn't. She'd convince him, once they were alone.

"It would still be a big task to find them," Jack said.

"Not if they haven't moved houses within the last twelve months. We had a census in April 1931, which contains all the information they could dream of," Aunt Mildred said.

"Then all they had to do afterwards was spy on the women and discover their routine," Frances said.

"I can't deny I'm relieved to see the role of the Athena Club was a coincidence. It wouldn't have been too difficult to notice the slipshod way the club is run and take advantage." Aunt Mildred ruffled Tink's ears.

"That reminds me. Dot wasn't afraid to let me see the recent invoices, so I assume they're all above board, but I did discover these entries in the accounts she kept locked in her desk drawer." Frances fished out her notebook. In the excitement over the death of the unknown veteran she'd all but forgotten about her snooping in the office.

Aunt Mildred studied them closely. "Not a single withdrawal under £500. Some of the names ring a faint bell. Hmm." She rang for her butler.

"My lady?" In he shimmered, just like the inimitable Jeeves Frances adored to read about.

"Please be so good as to tell my nephew we need his assistance."

"Very good, my lady." He stole away with so little noise that Uncle Sal watched him, mesmerised.

"Tommy's back?" Jack asked. Aunt Mildred's nephew, who relished playing sleuth as much as she did, had been absent from London for the last fortnight. He worked in some hush-hush capacity for Sir Reginald.

"He returned at noon, after 36 hours travel. I hope he can shed light on your notes, Frances."

With his blond hair slicked back and wet from a quick bath, the Honourable Tommy Clifton bounced into the room and greeted them profusely.

They'd quickly filled him in, and now he lounged with his feet on the metal bars surrounding the fireplace. Between swigs of a hot toddy to fight off a cold, he concentrated on Frances's writings.

"That's interesting," he said.

"Can you please be a little clearer?" his aunt asked.

"You were considering blackmail or embezzlement to explain the obvious attempts at cutting down expenses for the club." He took his feet off the metal bars and crossed his ankles, still stretched out luxuriously on his armchair.

"My mother-in-law says, it's been going on for almost two years. She thought it was due to the crash," Frances explained.

"I'd say so. Because this tells me someone's been playing fast and loose with the money. Remember when people in droves couldn't wait to sink their last penny into the stock market? Well, all the names Frances has listed here are connected to one of the bigger busts. I could be wrong, but it appears that your manageress threw good money after bad, trying to plug an ever-deeper hole."

"The club receives a yearly stipend," Aunt Mildred says.

"In what form? And who holds the purse strings? This definitely warrants a closer look."

Frances had a ghastly thought. "What if it's all connected? Dot needs money or she could be exposed and lose her job, or worse. And she has access to a typewriter."

"Then why wait this long to run a blackmail scheme?" Jack shook his head. "It also doesn't explain how she could have met our decidedly unsavoury villains. Both women said the letters had to be real because of the private information contained inside."

"I overlooked that." Tommy yawned. "Sorry, the old noodle isn't working too well yet. Lack of sleep."

"You've been bonzer," Frances assured him. "At least we have a good idea where the club's money went to."

Chapter 17

Sarah left her home after lunch. She'd dressed carefully, in a tweed skirt and jumper that were a little behind the fashion. If Poppy and Dash were still inclined to give them another refresher in jiu-jitsu, she was ready without having to worry about her clothes. It might appear callous to be this happy, considering that George had died, she thought, yet deep in her heart she only felt relief, for her own, and the baby's sake.

She hurried to catch the bus, smiling at all and sundry.

Her sunny mood lasted until she checked her pigeon-hole at the Athena. Inside, the all too familiar sight of an envelope chilled her to the marrow. She swayed. How was this possible?

"Are you all right?" For once, Dot guarded the reception desk. The bandage on her hand had been replaced by sticky plasters.

"Why, yes." Sarah willed herself to smile. "Is Katherine around?"

"I haven't seen her yet. You could give her a ring."

Sarah had to correct herself twice before she managed to give the operator the correct answer. With her free hand she held the door to the telephone cabinet closed. Her heart drummed so hard, she thought it might burst.

Thankfully, Katherine refrained from asking questions. She agreed without hesitation to stay in and wait for Sarah.

"Take a deep breath." Katherine ushered Sarah into the morning room, which at this hour was the warmest place in the flat. With the dog on a rug and the smell of freshly baked scones seasoning the air, the atmosphere was so homely that Sarah relaxed a little.

"Frances will be back soon. She's returning our books to the library," Katherine said. "If we wait, you won't have to tell your story twice. Unless it's something you'd rather my daughter-in-law doesn't hear about."

"No. You're lucky you get on so well."

Katherine smiled. "I couldn't ask for a better wife for my son."

They fell silent, until they heard the latchkey being turned in the lock.

"Sarah!" Frances clasped her hands. Katherine shot her daughter-in-law what looked like a warning glance. But why?

"Sarah's come to tell us something," Katherine said.

Sarah moistened her dry lips. "I went to the club, and there was this." She dropped the offending letter on the table, as if it burnt her fingers.

"Have you opened it?" Frances asked.

"Not yet."

Again, the envelope was addressed to Sarah Blake, written on a typewriter. The only difference to the earlier messages was the addition of the word Mrs.

"Shall I read it to you?" Katherine asked.

"Yes, please."

Katherine unfolded the single sheet of paper. "Dear Mrs. Blake, please receive my sincere condolences to your loss. But then I assume already having another husband will ease the pain of widowhood. I don't want to add to your burden, but George owed me money. To his landlady too, who might be tempted to come forward with your story if she doesn't receive what's rightfully hers. George spoke of you so much to both of us, we feel as if we know you already. One week should be enough for you to raise £20. Wait for instructions how to pay. Yours, a well-meaning friend"

Black dots danced in front of Sarah's eyes. That was the last she remembered.

When she came to, she rested on a divan, wrapped in a blanket. A kind elderly face peered at her. "How are you feeling, my dear? I'm Dr. Rawlings, by the way."

She blinked. The black dots had vanished. "A little light-headed," she admitted.

He clicked his tongue. "That's to be expected. I don't reckon there's much wrong with you, but I'd rather examine you. I've been told you're in the family way and have just had a nasty shock."

"Yes." She touched her belly.

"We'll be close by. Call out if you need anything, or ring the bell." Katherine indicated a cord, which presumably would have once been used to call the maid or a butler.

A lump formed in Sarah's throat. "Please stay."

"Of course." Katherine settled on a chair, within arm's reach.

Dr. Rawlings performed his duties in a reassuringly gentle manner. He spared Sarah questions about the nature of her shock, or anything else apart from talking about her eating habits and medical history.

"I haven't had much of an appetite lately," she admitted.

"A tonic will soon set that right." He wrote her a prescription. "You'll need to take things easy for a while. No rushing around or heavy carrying for you, young lady."

"I understand."

After the doctor had gone, Katherine insisted she rest a little longer. She and Frances had more questions about George, questions she could barely answer.

"Why does it matter which regiment he belonged to? He was wounded, at least once, and treated in a hospital in France. I remember him writing to me. He said he and his fellow soldiers were only there to be patched up, so they could be sent back to the front lines. Half of the letter was censored." She pressed her hands against her temples, willing herself to dredge up more memories.

"Did he have any particular friends he told you about? Or chums he enlisted with?" Katherine asked.

Sarah averted her gaze. Jack Sullivan had enlisted at the earliest moment and come all the way from Australia to fight. What would his mother and his wife think of her? "He didn't enlist. He always insisted that his work on the docks was too important to the war effort. George was conscripted in January 1916. Why does it matter?"

Did Katherine and Frances share a meaningful pause?

No, Sarah chided herself. She started to imagine things.

"Whoever wrote this new letter appears to have been well acquainted with George," Frances said. "If we have an idea where they met, he might be easier to identify."

A shiver ran down Sarah's spine. "You must think I'm a coward, but I don't know how much longer I can take this."

Katherine patted her hand. "You've been very brave so far, and now you're going to do exactly what the doctor told you. You'll stay at home and rest and leave everything else to us."

"I'd love nothing better, except that it's so horrible, lying to Harold. And what can you two do?"

Frances smiled at Sarah. "We'll figure it out. We always do."

Chapter 19

After shared memories over an excellent steak-and-kidney pie, washed down with a pint of bitter, Jack followed his guide through a maze of backyards. A few yards away from a flight of stairs leading down to a dark basement stood a couple of men. They were warming their hands over a fire burning in an old metal drum. Their woollen hats were drawn deep into their faces.

Jack had the sneaking suspicion that nothing went past these two.

Paul confirmed as much. "Ignore them."

"Why?"

"You'll see."

Downstairs, he knocked a tattoo on the door.

Slowly, it inched open.

"Password?" a voice demanded.

"Workers unite."

The door swung open, and Jack and Paul entered a dimly lit room. Tobacco smoke swirled in the air already pungent with boiled cabbage and paraffin oil. A red banner with hammer and sickle confirmed what Jack had already suspected. They'd come to a communist club.

"I hope you don't mind me taking you here," Paul said softly. "These men are your best bet when it comes to your man."

"No worries." Paul was right, Jack thought. He'd met enough commies to understand the appeal to soldiers returned from hell, only to find themselves again ignored and cast aside by the people they'd protected with their lives. The two blokes outside presumably stood watch in case the police took too close an interest.

He casually glanced around. On one table, a card game was in progress. On another, three men were engaged in a heated discussion regarding a recruitment poster for the party.

A samovar stood in the corner, where two women in coveralls handed out tea, with or without a dollop from a flask.

"There's a typewriter in the back room, use is for party members only. But it's not really enforced, and on an evening like this, you could easily sneak in. This is also the only crowd you can rely upon to cheer you on if you come out with an attack on the top brass," Paul told Jack in a low voice.

"Except for the officers who've seen the light and joined the ranks of the workers?" Jack had glimpsed a few likely candidates among the tea drinkers. It didn't surprise him. The longing for change had received new fuel when the economy crashed.

"We – they have also a few bright young things who've swapped society galas and nightclubs for protest marches."

"I gather you're a member?"

Paul blushed, as far as Jack could tell for sure without proper lighting.

"My girlfriend is. My cousin doesn't know. She's a little old-fashioned, when it comes to politics. Funny, because she used to be in the thick of the fight for the women's vote."

"Can you take me to the typewriter, or better yet, address an envelope for me? Mr. Basil Brown, courtesy of The Fountain, Hampstead Heath." The repeated letter B should be enough to show whether the blackmail letters had been typed in this building.

He waited less than five minutes for Paul to reappear with the envelope. As far as he'd observed, the door guard took his duty seriously, but like himself, anybody accompanying a person giving the correct password was welcome. Or George could have picked the code up while watching the club.

Jack considered that the most probable scenario. Only a fool would run unnecessary risks when setting out to commit a crime.

He took his leave from Paul, who deserved some privacy with his girlfriend, as far as that was possible given the surroundings. They agreed on another meeting. Meanwhile, Jack couldn't wait to return home and examine the envelope he'd acquired.

***

At her mother-in-law's, Frances fussed over Uncle Sal. He'd returned with a decided limp, and before she allowed him to do so much as utter a peep about his adventures, she insisted on his having a hot foot bath and a rum grog to ward off the chill.

That he gave in without protest told her he either silently admitted he was in pain, or he had the goods and didn't mind indulging her before he spilled the beans. Or both, she thought, as she saw the gleam in his eyes.

She brought the low pouffe from the morning room to sit close to him.

"That's better." He wiggled his toes in the shallow zinc bath they used to wash Leo in if he'd covered himself in mud. "I don't mind telling you that there's a lot to be said for having a car and a chauffeur. Mile after mile, I've been dragging my chain." He looked around. "Where is everyone?"

"Jack's not back yet. Katherine has gone to a meeting with her husband, so we can talk freely. Oh, I almost forgot there's a hot plate for you in the oven."

She jumped up, to fetch his dinner of gammon and chips.

"Wait a moment." He reached for the towel. "I'm not having my grub with a plate in my lap, like an invalid."

He was still tucking in when Jack burst through the door. "Where's —"

"Gone out," Uncle Sal interrupted him.

Both men eyed each other with excitement. "I'll fetch your plate, too, and then you two can tell your stories," Frances said.

"I had a quick bite with an old acquaintance."

Uncle Sal nodded at his hot toddy. "I could do with a refill, and I reckon it wouldn't hurt Jack either. It's the damp that does it."

"Coffee'll do me."

The kettle took forever to boil. Frances watched it with dismay. Maybe Jack and Uncle Sal had already tracked down the elusive George and were bursting to tell her. She also had a few things to contribute to their sleuthing. Still, she thought as she finally filled the coffee pot, the least she could do was take care of her menfolk's well-being.

"Let me." Jack took the tray from her and filled the cups. He remembered to add a spoonful of sugar for Uncle Sal and a splash of milk for her. Then he collected the magnifying glass and placed an envelope on the table.

"My old war mate got me this, from a private meeting place for communists. They have a typewriter in a back room."

Frances clapped her hands in amazement. "That's spiffing."

"It is," Jack agreed. He picked up the items and examined them. His face dropped. "Or rather, it would have been if I'd found the right place. Damn and blast."

Uncle Sal took on a smug air. "Never mind, Jack. I'll eat my old straw hat if you weren't on the right track after all. Because I've also made a new friend, and this joker swears there's a network of old soldiers, helping each other out. His brother got a new job like that, with someone answering advertisements for him, all spelled properly and typed as good as a letter from the palace, he said."

"Did he also mention the address?" Frances broke into a wide grin. "Too right you both did it."

"I couldn't probe too much," Uncle Sal said. "It was difficult enough coming up with chit-chat."

"I'll try Sam Finch. He should be able to at least point me in the right direction."

The fire burnt low. Frances yawned.

"I'd better push off," Uncle Sal said. "Mildred will be pacing a hole in her Persian rug by now."

"I'll see you home."

"No need, a taxi'll do."

He bent to kiss Frances's cheek. "Goodnight, sweetheart."

"Goodnight." She twinkled at him. "Wish us luck."

He crossed his fingers. "Why?"

"While you hunt George, we mustn't neglect the other half of the investigation. Tomorrow we'll invade the Athena Club good and proper."

Chapter 20

D ot stared aghast at Katherine, or rather, the leather trunk at her feet. "What on earth has happened?"

Katherine put on a brave face. "I promise I tell you once I'm installed in my room. Poppy and Dash told me they're leaving today, sooner than planned, and I'd surely be welcome to it instead."

"Certainly. That is, I'd have to consult the appointment book." Dot appeared rattled.

"Please," Katherine beseeched her.

Poppy and Dash bounded down the stairs. The man followed at a more sedate pace, lumbered as he was with suitcases and hat boxes.

"Katherine, darling." Dash clasped her hands. "We'll have to have a proper chinwag the next time. Such a frightful nuisance to be called away again at such short notice, but needs must, I'm afraid."

"I'd have said poppycock to all that, had it been anyone else but the vicar's wife. Imagine an elm tree crashing into the village hall! And the poor dear is struggling with all the arrangements and the insurance too."

"You'll sort it out in a jiffy." Katherine pecked the sisters on the cheek. "Frances will be sorry to have missed you."

Billy trod from one foot to another. Maybe had trouble standing too long, Katherine thought. Or he had other tasks to attend to, which caused him to grimace behind the sisters' back. She wondered fleetingly why Dot had hired him instead of a younger, more cheerful helper, until she remembered hearing they were related.

The arrival of the sisters' taxi hastened their goodbyes. "The room key." Dash slipped it into Katherine's hand. "All paid for in advance, for another three nights."

Katherine allowed herself a tiny smile. If she liked it or not, the manageress could hardly deny her the accommodation now.

The room on the first floor overlooked the street, including the entrance. Katherine listened for sounds. The traffic noise was a faint but constant background rumble. From the ground floor, voices drifted up, too low to be deciphered.

She flung her hat on the bed and motioned Billy to bring in her luggage.

"Thank you," she said as he placed it on the floor.

"Will that be all, Ma'am?"

She pressed a shilling on him. "It is for now."

Dot waited downstairs with the guest book. "If you'd be so good to fill in the registration?"

"Certainly." Katherine risked a quick glance at the earlier pages. The names tallied with guests she recollected. At least there was no fiddling with these accounts.

She felt a stab of shame. Only a week ago she'd put her hand in the fire for Dot's absolute honesty and here she was, ready and prepared to doubt everything and everyone.

"Tea?" Dot asked. "Then we can talk about what brings you here and what we can do to assist you in any way. You'll also need to be informed about our guest rules."

"Lovely."

Katherine let herself be installed in the breakfast parlour. It shared a wall with the kitchen, and the heat from the range seeped through.

She assumed that Dot tried to save coal and wood as much as possible. The room wasn't exactly chilly, but far from comfortable.

Dot brought the tea herself. "The upstairs maid's still not back, I'm afraid, so the parlour maids divide their time between the jobs."

"How vexing. There must be domestic agencies that could send you a girl for a week or so." No wonder the manageress had looked glum at the prospect of Katherine taking up residence.

Dot grimaced. "I'm afraid I have no choice. I only wonder if I should give the maid notice. If she's unable to return to work, I'll have to replace her. Such a shame. She's a good worker and most conscientious, with a widowed mother and young sisters depending on her."

"What did the doctor say?"

"He's afraid the lungs are affected. Luckily, it's not tuberculosis."

"We could have a collection, or a raffle, to support the girl's family while she recovers. Then you can use an agency to tide you over," Katherine suggested.

"You don't think the ladies would think it's an imposition, asking for their support?"

"Surely not. After all, that's the spirit in which the Athena Club was founded."

Dot's worry lines smoothed a little. "You're right. Enough of my worries, what is going on with you?"

They'd discussed Katherine's cover story in the morning. Marital problems had been dismissed, since people had long memories and loose lips, and Charles Parr didn't deserve to have his reputation shredded. The same went for trouble between Frances and Jack. In the end, they'd agreed on a simple explanation.

"Charles is away on business for a few days, so I have an opportunity to give my son and his bride a little bit of privacy. Not that there could be a more considerate young couple, but it can't be fun constantly having me under their feet. I'm sure you'll understand."

"I was wondering where Frances was."

"She'll still be around to assist you in whatever way she can," Katherine said.

"Let's hope I don't have to take advantage of her generosity. Now, for the house rules." The manageress rattled them off, with Katherine nodding in agreement. The arrangements couldn't have been better suited for her purposes. The front door was kept locked and bolted from eleven at night until eight in the morning. If a guest stayed out longer, they had to inform Dot in advance or ring the bell for the office. It also went through to Dot's flat in the attic and to Billy's private room at the back which had been converted from the old scullery.

"I assume you have the only keys. Or do you give out a spare?"

"Under no circumstances. I'm responsible for these premises and everything going on here. Why, if I handed over the keys, who knows who'd find their way in."

"What if you're going out yourself?"

"Then I give my residents ample warning. Midnight is the very latest when Billy will oblige and open the door, but I dare say you can be relied upon to be considerate."

"Absolutely. What about deliveries? I hope the milkman isn't rattling around at an ungodly hour."

"Seven o' clock on the dot and not a minute earlier. Breakfast's available from 7.30 am, and you already know lunch and dinner times."

Dot swept off, leaving Katherine to finish her tea.

A few hundred yards away, Tommy helped Aunt Mildred out of the limousine. An instant later, she held Tinkerbell in her arms while her nephew attached the leash to the dog collar. They were ready to join the investigation and do their bit of snooping around the Athena Club.

The corgi waited patiently until his mistress set him down and allowed him to sniff the trees.

Tommy tucked her arm under his as they set off for an innocent stroll. They both wished for a more active part, but scouting out the area accounted at least for something.

Sir Reginald had given Tommy the day off, and they'd jumped at the idea of assisting Jack and Frances.

Tinkerbell gave them an excellent excuse at stopping every few yards. Slowly, their goal came into sight. Although they agreed with Frances that the delivery entrance at the back was not the logical choice for the blackmailer or, more likely his errand boy, to have entered the club through, it nevertheless warranted a close look.

The street was quiet. Wrought-iron fences and gates with push-bells cordoned off small strips of lawn. Conservatories and the occasional playhouse for children were in keeping with the air of affluence that still hung about most houses. Two doors from the club, a woman scrubbed the doorsteps. She barely glanced up at them, another sign that she was used to seeing well-bred ladies and gentlemen around.

The club had a sign affixed to its gate. "For deliveries, ring twice."

Tommy casually tried the gate. "Locked," he whispered. A single-storey annex was tacked onto the back of the tall building. Curtains covered a small window. In the gap between them stood a potted cactus, a sign the annex was occupied.

They strolled around the corner, thus circling the club. A milliners' and a bookstore offered them an excuse to linger.

A notice in the window display of the bookstore caught Aunt Mildred's attention. "Room to rent, only quiet gentlemen need enquire."

She picked up Tink. "Let's have a look inside."

An elderly man was the sole occupant. He ran a feather duster over a shelf with used novels.

Tommy cleared his throat. The man dropped his duster.

"Sorry if I startled you," Tommy apologised.

"It's entirely my own fault, I assure you. I really need that shop bell seen to."

He blinked owlishly at Tommy. Tink yipped. "Well, hello there. What a splendid little fellow you are," the man greeted the corgi.

Aunt Mildred smiled. "You're a dog lover?" She signalled her nephew to leave the talking to her.

"I am indeed. Man's best friend, eh? Can't say fairer than that."

"Sadly, not all people agree. That's actually why we came inside. It says on your notice, you have a room to rent. My other nephew needs to move out of his lodgings for renovations, and he has a puppy. A beautiful corgi, but very young and quite shy. A place without too many other people bustling about would be ideal."

The man's eyes lit up. "Say no more. If you'd like to inspect the room? It's right above the shop. My own flat is on top. The bathroom would be shared by the two of us."

"Splendid."

A door led to a staircase, which was also accessible via the delivery entrance. A spacious room with comfortable furniture, including a small gas ring for heating a kettle offered everything Aunt Mildred had hoped for – including a window with a perfect view of the Athena Club.

"What do you think, Tommy? Will this do for your cousin and his dog?"

"I'd say it's jolly good."

"That's settled." She opened her purse. "I'd like to rent it for a week. How much do I owe you?

While the others were busy sleuthing, Jack and Sir Reginald shared a bench on the Embankment. "I can't keep this under wraps much longer," the older man said bluntly. "There's only so much interference the police will and should tolerate in a case of murder. If it wasn't the only chance to flush out the killer and to protect the ladies, they'd already have given the press a heads-up."

"How long do we have?"

"Two days. After that, the case goes public."

"Only 48 hours. That's not a lot."

"Chin up. I have seen you all work a miracle before. There's one more thing. The victim had his War Medal tucked away in his clothes. It was badly mangled by the car, but the name and part of the service number were still legible."

"A name." Jack expelled a deep breath. He hadn't realised how much the idea of a former soldier, murdered and going to an anonymous grave, had bothered him.

"Walter Piggott. He had no family that we were aware of. Simply one among the many who never really came home or had nothing to come home to. A few stints in hospitals, to treat shell-shock, that's all we can say for sure." Sir Reginald's jaw tightened.

Jack didn't ask why a member of the ruling class cared this much about this case. Some things were too personal.

Sir Reginald rose. "Give my regards to your wife, and don't forget, the clock is ticking."

Chapter 21

A War Medal. They'd been given out to every soldier who'd actively served in one of the many theatres of war. Jack's own were kept out of sight, in a box he'd closed in 1919 and not reopened. Most of his friends had done the same. They didn't need a reminder of the past.

Walter Piggott had clung to it. A foul taste crept into Jack's mouth. The man had deserved better, both in life and in death.

He shook off his unusual bout of despondency. Sir Reginald was right, they'd come up trumps before in seemingly hopeless cases. At least now he had a name to work with. He headed towards the tube.

He was still in his hat and coat when Frances breezed into the hallway of his mother's home. She carried a small suitcase and the dog bed.

"Is my mother kicking us out?" He hastened to take the things from her.

"As if she'd ever do that. It's only you who's moving, and Leo." She chuckled. "No worries, it's only during daytime and not for long. Oh, you'll need your camera and a good supply of film." She dashed off again.

He put down suitcase and dog bed and followed her. "Say that again."

"Aunt Mildred has found you the perfect recce spot. She say's it's got a bonzer view of the club entrance. All you need to do is take pictures of everyone who goes in, and once the next letter drops, we have a photograph of all the suspects." Her eyes shone with delight.

"That's a good plan, if a little unexpected." It also threw this own line of investigation into disarray. He'd have to rethink that.

"What about you? And what's my mother going to do?"

Katherine perched on a chair behind the Athena's reception desk. The latest copy of "Women's Weekly" kept her entertained, and if she spent less time studying the dress patterns and fashion advice and more time scanning her surroundings, nobody would notice.

"Are you sure you're comfortable?" Dot fretted. Katherine had run rough-shod over her and insisted on helping out.

"Of course. You worry too much. If the girl from the agency turns up, we don't want her to think the Athena isn't up to snuff, do we? And you've got more than enough on your hands."

"That's true and I'm already behind." Dot bustled off.

Katherine returned to her magazine.

She kept at the job until the lunch hour. It would have appeared odd had she declined to eat or insisted on having her saddle of mutton served at the desk.

Only five women occupied the dining room.

Katherine took a seat at Emily's table. The woman held up well, she decided. The only signs of turmoil were small starts at unexpected noises. Katherine said, "I'm quite looking forward to a few nights here. It's so peaceful, without the constant banging of doors and stream of deliveries one has to put up with in so many places." She hoped Emily would understand the message she tried to send her.

"It is marvellously quiet," another woman agreed. She speared a piece of potato. "And no husbands to hound you."

Her companion gasped. "You shouldn't say that. Why, you're lucky your man was too old to be called up. My Nancy would haven given anything to have her fiancé back, and I'm sure our dear Dot would agree."

"That's as may be, but I still hold it's nice to have a place of our own. A few hours at the Athena do us all a power of good. Even if the grub's a trifle repetitive lately."

Again, her companion chided her. "I'm sure we all appreciate cook and the rest of the staff. So reasonably priced too."

Katherine finished her meal. To her regret, she had to decline a cup of coffee. Duty called.

The Athena Club must be one of London's most solitary places, she decided two hours later. She'd accepted one flower delivery and one parcel from Woolworths, fielded two phone calls – one for Dot, the other for a guest – and taken down a message from the butcher's about a nice brace of game birds he had coming in.

She'd grown numb to Billy's passing through with his toolbox. She only wished he'd be less conspicuous. At least he'd been in the boiler room when the maid from the agency arrived. The woman was currently closeted with Dot.

Katherine fidgeted. If only something would happen.

Jack thought the same thing, in his new room across the street. He was grateful his membership in the photographic society had acquainted him with the best ways to take pictures from an angle, even in the washed-out light the lack of sunshine created, but the long lulls between visitors to the Athena were hard to fill in.

He didn't dare take a break from watching through the window either, and the puppy became restless.

Jack brought out Leo's favourite toy, a leather ball with tooth marks all over.

An Austin 7 pulled up outside the club. Jack twisted until he had a clear sight again. Two people exited the car. He focussed his camera lens. His finger rested on the shutter.

The couple went past the club. He swore under his breath. They had less than two days, and if this endeavour turned out to be useless, he might lose a better chance at exposing a murderer and blackmailer.

Leo dropped his ball and hunkered in front of Jack. "Sorry, mate." A quick glance told him the street lay deserted. He ruffled Leo's ears. "We'll go out as soon as possible."

The knock on his door coincided with the sight of his mother, stepping out onto the street.

"Your relief, at your service." Tommy gave him a salute. "Show me what I have to do and then you're free to toddle off for a while."

Jack handed him Leo and the leash. "Take him to the nearest public square. I'll be with you in a twinkle."

"The game is on?"

"I sincerely hope so." He pointed to the window, where Katherine was clearly visible.

Tommy tapped his nose. "Say no more."

Jack packed his used rolls of film with as much care as if they'd been a babe in arms. These inches of celluloid might hold the key to their investigation.

He caught up with Tommy and Katherine a quarter mile away. Leo sniffed at every bush.

Katherine huddled into her coat. "Finally. I can't stay out too long. I'm needed for a rubber of bridge."

"I assume the letter's arrived?"

"Two, one for Sarah and one for Emily."

"Did you see who delivered them?"

She shook her head. "It happened while I'd gone to powder my nose. I can't have left the desk for more than five minutes. If you've been on the spot —"

"Trust me, I was."

"Then all you need to do is develop your images and deliver them to your Sir Reginald Fitzpatrick."

"The chief will be pleased," Tommy chimed in. "Rather ingenious, if I may say so."

"Except, when did you go and powder your nose?" Jack asked Katherine, half dreading her reply.

She shot him a bewildered look. "Right before I left the club. I returned, checked the pigeon-holes - don't you worry, I used my mirror and pretended to inspect my hair. Then I grabbed my coat and dashed outside. Why? Have I made a blunder?"

"There was not a single soul who entered the Athena during the last half hour."

Her mouth fell open. "I don't understand. I thought we'd ruled out ..."

"An inside job. Gosh." Tommy said.

"You need to go back. I'll ring you up at the club," Jack told his mother.

"It has to be before ten, or the doors will be locked." She left, looking as defeated as he felt.

"What now?" Tommy asked.

"Do you have the car nearby?" Jack enquired.

"Yes?"

"Fetch Uncle Sal. Tell him he's a man recently come over from Australia, searching for his nephew. There's a bit of money waiting for the lad." He handed Tommy a piece of paper with a few notes about

Walter Piggott. "He can begin his search at The Crown and Anchor. He's to find anyone who's seen Piggott with someone else or heard about him having a bit of work offered."

"Is that the dead man?"

Jack nodded.

"What's my role?" Tommy asked.

"You hang around and guard Uncle Sal's back. We might be stirring up a hornet's nest here."

"I won't let you down."

Chapter 22

At Aunt Mildred's, Frances sat, dumbstruck. If Tommy's hasty recounting of events was true, where did it leave them?

The young man paced like a caged tiger as he waited for Uncle Sal.

His aunt quirked an eyebrow at him. "Impatience doesn't make seconds pass faster. What it does is cloud your thinking."

"Dash it, I mean, it's a huge responsibility, and I could do with a few pointers about my role. Is it, not so smart young toff stumbles into boozer? I could be mildly tipsy. Or do I pretend to wait for a chum? Or brace myself for an unpleasant visit? What do I wear? Flannels and blazer and an overcoat, or evening dress? It all comes natural to Uncle Sal, I suppose, but I'm a beginner at this cloak and dagger stuff."

"You'll do alright, old boy." Uncle Sal had chosen the perfect moment for his entrance. Horn-rimmed spectacles, with lenses of window glass, and a waxed moustache changed his appearance completely. Sheepskin-lined gloves and two pullovers worn on top of each other, plus a caped raincoat and bronzed skin played into the idea of a recent stint in the antipodes. Those boxes of garments Aunt Mildred had purchased had proven a winner, Frances thought.

Uncle Sal clapped his hand on Tommy's shoulder. "A soft collar, with a stud undone, and a soft hat, if you have one at hand, should do nicely. Then all you need to do is act a bit nervous, like, and mutter something about becoming an uncle. Your sister's confined nearby, and the doctor sent you packing because you're in the way."

"Uncle or father?" Tommy cheered up.

"Uncle. New fathers tend to be the centre of attention. You don't want to be bombarded with questions. If you stand everyone a round, once I'm ready to leave, it should let us slip away easily."

"I can work with that." Tommy had a new spring in his step as Frances waved them goodbye.

Aunt Mildred played with a tapestry-frame. A needle-work box stood on a side-table, yet Frances had never watched her in action. She'd assumed it to be a prop, like Uncle Sal's spectacles. If people saw what they expected to see, they let their guard down so much more easily, and a lady and needlework went well together.

"Letting their guard down," she whispered.

"Pardon?" Aunt Mildred asked.

"I need to go out, to see Sarah. I'll soon be back."

"Not on your own, while there's a murderer on the loose. Jack would never forgive me if I let you out of my sight."

On Aunt Mildred's insistence, they took a brief detour to pick up a hamper with tea, beef tea, and biscuits.

To Frances surprise, her friend proved herself to be adept at manoeuvring the limousine through the London traffic.

Aunt Mildred giggled. "You didn't think I'm capable of doing more than regally sitting in the back, barking orders? Dear Tommy, it pleases him so much to chauffeur me that I don't want to spoil his fun."

The arrival of a smart car, driven by an expensive-looking lady no less, caused a stir in the street where Sarah lived.

Aunt Mildred ignored the curious stares of both children and housewives and swept ahead, Frances plus hamper in her wake.

She rang the doorbell.

Loud steps clattered down the staircase. A hatchet-faced woman opened. "What is it yer wanting?"

"Visiting yer 'ighness," a scallywag called out.

Aunt Mildred used her pince-nez to its full effect, silencing the boy.

"We're here to see Mrs. Todd," Frances said.

The hatchet-faced woman glowered at her. "It says ter ring twice for Todd, not once. And me 'aving ter come running, with me bad leg."

A coin gleamed in Aunt Mildred's hand. "So sorry to have troubled you."

The woman swooped up the coin. "I'll jest run up, real quick-like, and tell Mrs. Todd as she 'as visitors."

They followed the woman at a sedate pace.

Sarah stood in the door, wrapped into a warm flannel. Her colour changed as she recognised Frances. "Please come in."

The hatchet-faced woman beat a retreat.

"Don't be alarmed," Aunt Mildred said. "We only wanted to keep you informed and see how you're keeping up."

"Harold will be home soon. He's only fetching a few things for supper." Sarah swayed as she took them through to the living room.

"Have you eaten at all?" Frances asked.

"I've tried, but I could only swallow a morsel."

"A strong cup of beef tea is what you need." Aunt Mildred searched through the hamper. "There it is."

Meekly, Sarah followed them to the kitchen where Frances took over. While she waited for the water to heat, she asked the question that had occupied her mind ever since she thought of it. "Have you ever talked about George, at the club or at least with another member?"

"Why, no. That is – only once. The parlour maid had knocked over the teapot. So stupid, really, but it spilled on my silk jumper and burnt my skin. I had to take off the jumper, or it would have stained, and Emily noticed —" She broke off.

"What did she notice?" Frances fixed the beef tea.

Sarah took a careful sip. She held out her arm and pushed back her sleeve. Above her wrist was an ugly scar. "This. The tea hadn't scalded me too badly, although they insisted on treating it with ointment and a bandage, but somehow it all came flooding back. The screaming, the threats, and the way he used to take out his anger on me. I said I was glad when he was declared missing. Glad, glad, glad, and I didn't need a death certificate to feel free." She took another sip. Her voice became stronger. "Emily asked, your husband was also never formally identified? Then, somebody closed the door, and we shut up. We never spoke about it again."

"Emily Pennington?"

"Yes. She's another war widow."

"Did George and her first husband know each other?"

"I have no idea. Why?"

Aunt Mildred opened her mouth to speak. A key turned in the lock.

Frances signalled her to be quiet. "Everything's going to be fine. You get your rest now."

They took their leave after a quick introduction to Harold, who was more concerned with his wife's well-being than with visitors, despite Aunt Mildred's title. Frances took to him in an instant. After the hell her first husband had put her through, Sarah had chosen wisely on her second attempt.

"Home?" Aunt Mildred started the engine.

"Please. We need to ring up Katherine before it's too late."

Chapter 23

U ncle Sal rubbed his hands as he shuffled into The Crown and Anchor. Tommy lounged in a corner, with a clear view of the pub room. He had a barely touched drink in front of him and displayed a nice mix of nervousness and bonhomie, if Uncle Sal was any judge.

He steered to the bar. "Perishin' cold tonight. Does you good to come inside." He eyed the tap. "Ale for me, please."

"Coming up." The landlord filled a glass to the brim, wiping off the overflow.

"That's what you call cold? Why, there's barely a nip in the air," barrel-chested man said with disdain.

"For you it might be balmy, but if you're used to proper sunshine, it ain't, mate." Uncle Sal exaggerated his Australian accent. He took a deep swig.

"We'll have another freeze yet. I can feel it in me bones," another man said. He tapped his stiff leg. "Better than a barometer, me bones."

"Where are you from then?" the landlord asked.

"Australia, these last 30 years. I don't mind telling you, I miss the heat on my skin. But once you get on in years, there's nothing like the old home. And the beer, too." He admired the golden liquid.

"Australia? That's mighty far," the stiff-legged man said.

"I came over a little while ago. Not many of my old cobbers still around, but I was hoping to find my nephew. On the wife's side, he is. I promised her on her deathbed I'd look him up, here in London. There's a few things she wanted him to have. Family heirlooms, like."

"Any luck?" the landlord asked.

"Not yet. I was hoping one of you gents might be of assistance."

"Us?" The barrel-chested man gaped at him.

"I was told I'd find a few of his soldier mates here." Uncle Sal mentioned the regiment.

"That's my old outfit alright," the man with the stiff leg said.

"Mine too," another man said. The bloke next him nodded as well.

"That's bonzer. The name's Walter Piggott. Last we heard, he'd been demobbed."

"That's a mighty long time," the barrel-chested man said.

"He's never been much of a letter writer, leastways with us, and neither was my missus," Uncle Sal admitted. "Do you know him?"

The veterans exchanged glances Uncle Sal couldn't decipher. Was it wariness or guilt?

"He was a good lad," one of the men said.

"Was?" His pulse quickened. While the newspapers had carried a brief notice about a fatal accident, the body hadn't officially been identified. Any person aware that Walter Piggott was dead, had to be involved with his demise.

"He changed, since he lost his job a few years back. A docker, that's what he was for a while, but his chest gave him too much trouble."

"Mustard gas was what did it, same as my brother," another man chimed in.

"He drops in once in a while, when he's got a few shillings in his pocket, but I haven't seen him around in a while," the landlord confirmed.

"Does he have mates he's especially friendly with?" Uncle Sal asked.

"He kept himself to himself, mostly, after things went bad for him." The stiff-legged man scratched his head. "I reckon you could ask around at the service-men's association."

"More likely, he'll go to our own outfit," the barrel-chested man suggested.

"That's true. It's not official, like the British Legion, but darn useful it can be. If I were you, that's where I'd go."

A few miles away, Jack caught up with Sam at the end of his delivery round. "That's thirsty work," he said.

"That it is. Makes my evening tipple taste that much sweeter."

"I can imagine. Fancy joining me for a drink?"

Sam hesitated.

"Or is the wife waiting with your tea?"

"She won't mind, if I leave her notice. It's her day at her mum's. Only, I'm a bit grubby."

"Nothing a bit of water won't fix."

With Sam's face and hand cleaned of coal dust, he declared himself ready to go with Captain Jack wherever desired.

"The thing is, I'd like to pick your brain." Jack paused at a Lyons Corner House. "Will this do?"

"I won't say no to that."

Over beer, bangers and mash, and the background noise of a string quartet, Jack confided in Sam. "Seeing you again and what's going on with our old mates has me thinking there must be more I can do back home. I employ as many of my men as I can, but there's only so many jobs at the Top Note. What do you do here to support each other? Rely on the British Legion and the Service Men's Association?"

"Not blimmin' likely, if you pardon my French. There's too many of us in need, and not all up to jumping through hoops. What we do is to try and fill the gaps. We've got an office, casual only, but it's doing the trick."

"An office?"

"I'll show you."

The office surprised Jack. He'd expected a back room of sorts. Instead, Sam took him to a well-lit place on the second floor of an office building. The key was kept hidden in an umbrella stand.

"Aren't you afraid of burglars?"

"There's nothing much to steal. The metal cabinets weigh a ton, and the typewriter's chained to the floor."

"Clever idea." Jack examined the chain. It consisted of two halves, joined by a padlock. One half was indeed bolted to the floor and the other was soldered to the body of the machine. "I assume if it needs fixing, you'll open the padlock and away you go."

Sam knocked on wood. "Yeah. So far, we haven't had any problems, I'm happy to say."

"Who uses the typewriter? Is it open to anyone?"

"Good grief, no. Or we'd go through a dozen ribbons a month. It's like this, once a week we have a real typist coming in, the daughter of one of our sergeants. She does an evening. Then we have a day where a private gives up his lunch break. He's a clerk, so he's a wiz at typing and he also knows all them fancy words you'd wish for."

"Only those two are allowed to touch the typewriter?"

"We've got one or two more who have the right touch with it, and if we're hard-pressed they gets roped in."

"How does your system work?" Jack itched to see a typed sample. He also genuinely wanted to hear more about this informal support network.

"It's like this." Sam opened the doors of the metal cabinet and pulled out two ledgers.

"If you want a letter written, you'll log it here. Then you give your name, the date, and if you come in personally or leave handwritten details in the in-tray. That's kept in the drawer."

"And the other ledger?"

"That's our visitor's book. Again, you write your name and date, and the reason. If you're searching for work, it goes in there, and what kind of work. Then there's a column for results, jobs applied for and if you were called in for an interview. We have a separate book for reviews, so we have a bit of an insight what certain employers are like and what they want or don't want."

Jack opened the visitor's book. "You seem busy." He scanned the columns. There. Black on white, he saw the name Walter Piggott, appearing at least once a month. "Any work considered."

"Do you work together with an employment agency?" Jack asked.

"We've come up with our own system. See this?" Sam opened another drawer. Job advertisings cut from newspapers filled a box. "Every evening, those of us with access to the papers cut out the stuff and the next day, they drop it off or have someone else bring it in. Then it's back to our ledger, to see if we have a suitable candidate. And if anyone hears of a job going, say as a delivery boy or a man or a cleaner, what doesn't get advertised, he makes a special note of it."

"Great stuff. That'd work in Adelaide just as well as it does here in London. That is, I assume it does the trick? This Piggott here and a few others don't appear to have been too lucky."

"It's hard times for everyone. I remember having heard something about Piggott finally having found work."

Jack studied the ledger again, trying his best to appear casual. No mention of George Blake in these pages.

Then, his heart skipped a beat. Sam showed him the small stash of already typed letters, waiting to be collected. The capital B was missing a bit.

He'd found the typewriter.

Chapter 24

At the pub, Uncle Sal grinned at his new friends. "You've been very helpful. How about a round to say thank you?"

"Hear, hear," said one of the men.

When the beer stood on the counter, he dropped another question. "I recollect Walter mentioning one particular cobber in his letters. George, that was the name. George Blake."

The jovial atmosphere changed.

"Him?" The stiff-legged man spat out the word.

In his corner, Tommy fidgeted.

Uncle Sal frowned. "What's wrong with him?"

"Let's say, George Blake didn't have many friends, apart from Carl and William. Hoping for a blighty wound, they all did, and if it hadn't become too dangerous, they'd have shot themselves in the foot."

"Can't say I blame them," a hitherto quiet man said. "We all dreamed of being sent home, didn't we?"

A blighty wound, Uncle Sal remembered, was an injury that led to being prevented from any further combat, without crippling or seriously hurting the victim. Once the numbers of these wounds were rising, the powers that be had ordered court-martials for any soldier suspected of having suffered a self-inflicted wound.

"But none of us would have used our mates for cover, like George Blake did. Talking all tough about slapping around the wife, and then soiling his pants when he came under fire. I don't recollect him being friendly with Walter Piggott."

"Anyway, if my nephew turns up, tell him, his Australian uncle's in town." He gave them all a quick goodbye and took his leave.

He waited around the corner for Tommy, who arrived five minutes later. The young man was flushed with excitement. "That was brilliant. You've found the connection."

"You weren't doing too badly yourself. Blending right into the woodwork."

"You're a good teacher. And you had them talking about that George fella even after you left."

"They did? What did they say?"

"Only that nobody's clapped eyes on him since before the battle where he went missing. There's one or two swearing to it that he deserted, and that he might have had help."

*****

"There's a phone call for Mrs. Parr? Your daughter-in-law, the lady said she is." The new upstairs maid waited respectfully for Katherine to rouse herself from the chair and follow her.

Katherine hid her nervousness. She'd been on tenterhooks since Jack had squashed all their earlier theories. "Yes?"

She listened to a torrent of words. "Slow down, please, my dear." To her relief, Frances took a deep breath and started again. Katherine's chest tightened so much it hurt as she finally grasped what her daughter-in-law suggested, and why they had no choice.

Slowly, she pushed the door of the telephone cabinet open, and half stumbled outside.

"Good heavens, Katherine, what's wrong? You're white as a sheet." Dot, bless her, appeared just in time to steady Katherine.

"I've had a bit of a shock, I must admit." She dragged herself to the most comfortable seat in the lounge. It had the added benefit of a sticking door which allowed conversations to be overheard from the hallway. With a few members still around, it didn't afford much privacy, but a woman as distraught as Katherine pretended to be, could easily overlook that.

Dot chafed her hands. "Is there anything I can do for you?"

"Maybe a small brandy? And a bit of advice."

"I'll be with you in a tick."

True to her word, Dot hurried back with two tumblers. Katherine clung to her drink, doing her best to remember Uncle Sal's demonstrations of a stage whisper. She had to make eavesdropping easy.

"You're not drinking," Dot said.

Katherine gulped half the brandy down. It burnt in her throat. She coughed.

Dot swigged hers without an adverse reaction. "You said you wanted advice."

"It's silly, really, when you think of it. A lot of water under the bridge too, and nothing I could change, even if I wanted to," Katherine mused.

"You lost me."

"I left a box with old photographs out for Frances and Jack, but I forgot that I'd kept a few letters and documents in there as well." She downed the rest of her brandy, this time without coughing. "How could I be so stupid?"

Dot patted Katherine's hand again. "It can't be that bad, whatever it is."

"If only. If only I can make her understand that what I've done was only telling a little white lie. It didn't hurt anyone."

Dot's brows shot up in surprise.

Katherine took a deep, dramatic breath. "When I returned home to England, I let everyone know I'd been given a divorce from my first husband, in Australia."

"There's no shame in that," Dot said, although Katherine thought she detected a note of reproach in her tone.

"Exactly. And I would have been granted the divorce if the brute hadn't used the opportunity to go bush. As matters stood, I had to take things into my own hands."

"You're not divorced after all?"

"Only not in the eyes of the law. In every other aspect, I cut ties with Jack's father long ago. Charles Parr is my real husband."

"What a dilemma," Dot said.

"How can I convince Frances that it's only a formality and there's no reason for her to create a fuss or to tell my son and husband? Because if she does, it might tear my family apart." She pulled out a linen handkerchief and blew her nose.

"That's a serious issue," Dot said. "I wish you hadn't told me."

"But you're on my side, right?"

"The law —"

"Is wrong. It's been wrong before and will be wrong again. Only a few generations back we would have been the property of our fathers or husbands, completely at their mercy. You fought side by side with our sisters for the vote, and for equal rights. What should I have done, let a man who didn't care a fig about me or our children, ruin our lives? No. No."

A wan smile crept onto Dot's face. "That's what you should tell your daughter-in-law."

"You're right. She promised to keep quiet for 48 hours. By then I'll have come up with a plan. Thank you, Dot."

New optimism surged through Katherine as she retired to her room.

Chapter 25

In the meantime, Aunt Mildred entertained an unexpected visitor. Tink decided to divide his lavish affection between Tommy and Sir Reginald. Uncle Sal was still in the bath.

Frances suppressed the urge to offer the aristocratic guest a clothes brush. She'd grown used to removing dog hair from their clothes on a daily basis, but Sir Reginald's personal servant might be in for a surprise.

"That's enough, Tinkerbell," Aunt Mildred said in a stern voice as he decided to climb onto Sir Reginald's lap.

"Good boy." Sir Reginald sat the corgi down.

"I'd take him for a walk, except I assume I might be needed here. Unless you've only come to pay my aunt a strictly social visit," Tommy said to his superior.

"As delightful as that would be, you've guessed correctly."

"Jack said we have more than a day left," Frances said, bewildered.

"I've been hoping to find him here, actually."

"He'll soon be back."

"Then we'll wait with our discussion and this little fellow can enjoy his evening constitutional."

"A short round will do. Take Leo as well," Aunt Mildred told her nephew.

He whistled. "Come on, Tink, Leo."

The puppy woke with a start.

"I'll join you," Frances said. All this sitting still and waiting was agony. At least walking the dogs would provide a distraction.

Tommy took care to match his steps to hers. He seemed more excited about his adventures sleuthing than he did about his comfortable life as one of Sir Reginald's promising underlings. "What would you have done if you hadn't been born with money and a title?" she asked.

"I'm not that rich and younger sons aren't that special," he defended himself.

"I didn't mean that as criticism. Only, there seem to be so many things that are expected of you. Following in footsteps and so on. At least, that's my impression."

"Clever girl. I can't complain, not by a long shot, but there are moments I wish I could be like Jack. Free to forge my own way and do what I really want."

"He does shoulder an awful lot of responsibility," she retorted.

"As do you. Where all I'm supposed to do is to mingle with all the right people, visit all the right places, and not utter a single original thought for fear of ruffling some feathers."

"Not Aunt Mildred's feathers though."

"Heavens, no. She's a good egg. Worth a dozen of my other relatives, even if she thinks I'm hopelessly susceptible to a pretty face and a sad story." He broke off with an embarrassed grimace. "Let's go back."

Jack was already waiting. He pulled her next to him. "We have a full council of war, it appears. Who goes first? Sir Reginald?"

"With pleasure. I've followed the trail Tommy uncovered, regarding the financial affairs of the club."

Frances had forgotten about that. How stupid, she thought.

Sir Reginald continued. "The money Lady Pemberton left the Athena Club is supervised and managed by a board of trustees consisting of three members. Each of them is allowed to sign off on financial transactions. This stipulation allows the seamless functioning in cases of illness or other reasons why a member might be unavailable when a sudden need for action arises."

"So, the board holds the purse strings?" Jack asked.

"It does. Its members are Lady Pemberton's old solicitor, who's pushing eighty if he's a day, and two leading lights of the suffragist movement."

"Then who invested the money in the stock market? It can't have been Dot, at least not without permission," Frances said.

"Yes and no. The original suggestion came from a board member, one who'd sprung the manageress from prison when the police arrested several dozen women during a protest march."

"That would explain who authorised the transactions but not the current penny-pinching, unless there are huge loans to repay." Aunt Mildred pursed her lips.

"There aren't. I got the impression that your Dot is trying valiantly to protect her benefactress's reputation, at all costs."

"Even at the cost of blackmailing the women she's there to serve? Because the letters are delivered by someone on the inside, and she has all the private information about the victims available."

"Are you sure?" Sir Reginald asked Frances.

"We've confirmed that."

"But she can't have killed Walter Piggott. She was on duty at the Athena during the crucial hours, if I'm not mistaken," Sir Reginald said.

"She didn't have to. It was a man alright, and I'll eat my hat if he isn't the one supplying the letters. I've found the typewriter." Jack's words caused a well deserved stir, Frances thought.

"You really haven't wasted a second," Sir Reginald said.

"It could have been George Blake," Uncle Sal chimed in. "Or more likely, one of his mates. He wasn't exactly well-liked among the other men, but there were two men he was friendly with. I got the impression they both made it back from the front and they might have been the ones helping him make a run for it."

"That narrows it down tremendously." Sir Reginald rubbed his hands. "We'll figure out who it was after all."

"We might not have to," Frances said.

"What's that?" Jack stared at her.

Frances's mouth went dry. "You were already gone, so we thought it best to prepare a trap before Sir Reginald takes us off the case."

"A trap?"

"We know the blackmailer's desperate for money, or greedy, or both. So, we thought if we offer him another, easy victim —" she stopped.

"Who did you rope in?" Jack glared at her.

Her next words came out as a croak. "Your mother."

Chapter 26

The next morning the nearby church bells roused Katherine from an uneasy sleep. She stared in the mirror of her washstand. Had those deep lines on her forehead been there yesterday? At least she didn't need to use artificial means to look like a nervous wreck when she went down, she thought.

If only she had an excuse to talk to Jack or Frances. She did some limbering exercises, to calm herself. One wrong move could ruin everything. All she had to do was keep her wits about her and play her role for a little while longer.

She waited as long as possible before she went down for breakfast, deliberately ignoring the reception area.

The parlour maid cleared the big table. She bobbed a curtsy. "Good morning, Ma'am. What can I bring you?"

Katherine chose a table by the window. "Coffee, please. Toast with marmalade and a soft-boiled egg will do."

The same two women who'd discussed husbands before waved at her on their way out. She raised her hand in a vague greeting.

Finally, she was alone.

"Your breakfast, Ma'am. Will that be all?"

"Thank you. It all looks splendid."

The maid bobbed another curtsy and dashed off. Katherine buttered her second piece of toast when from upstairs, she heard the rumbling of the vacuum cleaner. The early post had been delivered while she was still in bed, and the morning newspapers lay on a side table.

She fought with herself if she should read it or not, for the sake of verisimilitude. As tempting as it was to keep an eye on her pigeon-hole, she couldn't afford to give away her interest.

Katherine turned the pages to the classified ads. Half an hour, she told herself. That should be long enough.

She took her breakfast tray to the kitchen herself. It saved the maid a small task, thus keeping in line with Katherine's amply demonstrated helpfulness. It also allowed her a glimpse of something in her pigeon-hole.

Katherine fished out the letter without a second glance and stuffed it carelessly into her purse. Any watcher could find nothing suspicious about that, she decided, just like returning to her room before setting out was only to be expected.

She opened the curtains and closed them again, as a signal for Jack. She imagined him watching her window from across the street since the crack of dawn. Now, for the message she'd received.

It was addressed to Mrs. Katherine Sullivan, sadly lacking the tell-tale B. She slit the envelope open with a penknife.

What about fingerprints? If the letter became evidence, her prints might cover the writer's prints, she thought. Why didn't crime novelists give one detailed advice? On the other hand, she assumed murderers and thieves and blackmailers also studied the works of Agatha Christie, Dorothy L. Sayers, and Edgar Wallace with the greatest interest.

With her hands in her warm leather gloves, she slid out the letter and read it. "Does your new husband know he married a bigamist? A donation of £50 for a good cause might ease your conscience and buy you the silence of Mr. Sullivan's friends. Instructions will follow. Be aware that it's not only you who has to otherwise suffer consequences."

She held the letter up to the light. The B was missing a fraction. Whereas the other letters had shown personal knowledge of the victims, this was a pure attempt at extortion. With pretty much nothing known here in England about Jack's father, the blackmailer had nothing to go on. She returned the letter to the envelope and sat down to write a note of her own.

Once outside, she hurried towards the shops. She'd be safe in broad daylight, among other people. Nevertheless, she kept as far from the kerb as possible. If the blackmailer followed her, he'd see a nervous woman. Cold sweat beaded her forehead. Not much further now until her destination.

On the other side of the road, Jack kept his box camera on the windowsill. Instead of its lens, he trained a powerful set of binoculars on the club. Aunt Mildred used them for birdwatching in the countryside, but they worked as well in the city. He'd spent the night in his new lodgings, the first night without his wife. He missed her, although they'd come close to their first row about her undiscussed plan to use his mother as bait. Only the facts that it was their best shot, and that they were running out of time had cooled his temper.

His stomach rumbled. He wolfed down a sandwich, prepared by Aunt Mildred's cook and sent along with a thermos flask with tea. Jack could sleep in any situation, a knack he'd learned during the war, and he also woke up at will. Thus, he'd started his surveillance before the first delivery boys and messengers swarmed out.

He'd seen the curtains in his mother's room move. Now, he watched her leave, without glancing over her shoulder. That was good, he thought. All she had to do was keep her nerve a little longer.

A man in a grey coat and hat came into sight, leaning on his cane. For a heartbeat, Jack tensed. A cane could easily be used to trip up a person and push them in front of a car. There was no way Jack could reach them before the man caught up with Katherine.

Then he relaxed. The man had twirled his cane in a manner as familiar to Jack as the back of his hand. Uncle Sal acted as bodyguard.

Frances had positioned herself in a nearby tea-room. She said a silent prayer. Her plan had been so quickly cobbled together that she might have made a blunder. If only she'd had the chance to talk it through with Jack, before she involved his mother. She'd seen the surprise and the rising fear he worked so hard to suppress. If anything happened to Katherine, he'd never forgive her, nor would she be able to forgive herself.

They'd been in tricky situations before, but always together, working as a team.

As quick on the uptake and spirited as her mother-in-law was, Katherine was a middle-aged woman, unused to dealing with criminals. Where was she?

Only when Katherine turned around the corner did Frances breathe freely. She left her convenient window spot and took her bill to the cashier.

Katherine's steps echoed on the marble floor of the bank. Although she was fairly certain she hadn't been followed, she intended to stick to every detail of the plan.

The blackmailer demanded £50, a sum that most members of the Athena Club would be hard pressed to come up with. Without a nest-egg or at least an account that allowed them to withdraw money without express consent from a husband, most women could only lay hands on the house-keeping money.

The £15 Katherine took out of her account were the biggest sum she'd withdrawn in years. The crisp £1 notes seemed to burn a hole in her purse. Still, it wasn't enough by far.

Her next stop took her further towards the West End. Three golden balls above a door signalled a pawnbroker. She'd visited this establishment before, with a friend.

The pawnbroker greeted her with the discretion of a man used to dealing with pillars of society and members of the upper class, who were anxious to get hold of large sums of money for a short while.

She took off her pearl earrings and matching choker, both a wedding gift from Jack. It pained her to part with them, however short it would be.

Fake pearls had become all the rage a few years ago, so she waited patiently while the pawnbroker used a loupe to examine every single pearl to ensure they were the real thing. "Very nice. An unusual shade of champagne colour. It's not often to see South Sea pearls of this quality."

"I only intend to be without them for a brief time," she said.

"Naturally." He studied her clothes and shoes. They were of decent quality but not in the same league as her precious pearls. He'd offer her a lower sum than he'd originally planned, she assumed. It didn't matter, as long as she pawned the pearls. For a fleeting moment she toyed with the idea of stopping the transaction. Surely her entering the shop would satisfy any watcher.

Then she thought of Sarah and her unborn baby, and of Emily, and of the veteran who must have thought his luck had finally turned for the better, only to be murdered in cold blood.

With that in mind, she accepted the offer and terms without blinking. She stashed away the bank notes in an envelope he kindly offered her.

"That's a lot of money to carry around," he said. "I wonder —"

"Yes?"

"I don't want to frighten you, Ma'am, but your handbag is an easy target and if you leave our kind of establishment, it's fair to say that pickpockets might pick up the scent, so to say. It's odds on that you'll carry cash or other valuables."

Her heart sank. She hadn't considered that people other than the blackmailer observed places of interest.

The pawnbroker had a suggestion. "If you'd pin the envelope to the lining of your coat, unless it has an interior pocket, that'd keep the money safe."

She accepted a safety-pin. "That's very kind."

"Anything to keep our customers happy."

With a small fortune hidden in her coat, Katherine pressed on. She risked a pause outside a shop window, to open her handbag and produce a handkerchief.

Uncle Sal ambled past. She only recognised him because of the tune he whistled. The cavalry hadn't deserted her.

She snapped the handbag shut, blew her nose in a discreet, ladylike manner, and stowed away the handkerchief in her coat pocket before she set off again.

After what felt like an eternity but in reality took less than an hour, Katherine slipped into a Victorian villa in a sad state of neglect. Though still in London and only a few minutes from the tube station, there wasn't a single person close by.

Inside, boxes upon boxes crammed with outdated clothes, worn furniture, and battered wooden toys took up most of the big room. A large wardrobe stood against a wall. Katherine tapped on the doors. With a creak, the door swung open. "The hinges need a drop of oil," Frances said as she climbed out.

Katherine hugged her as tight as she could. "Be careful, darling girl."

"I will."

Chapter 27

Frances wished she'd had the foresight to spend last night dusting the place. Her nose tickled and her eyes itched, yet she didn't dare move.

Had they really thought of everything? What if the note had failed to lure their prey? "I KNOW WHO YOU ARE. I will make the suggested purchase only if you you give me a written guarantee and receipt." The address and time of day she'd added had been carefully selected to allow a secluded meeting at dusk, to add to the blackmailer's sense of security.

She wiggled around. If he came, he'd see all the goods waiting to be sorted, restored, and distributed to the deserving poor by one of Aunt Mildred's charitable groups.

Katherine's hat was visible from the door. Its wearer occupied a three-seater sofa, covered with a floor length throw. A side table held a half-eaten sandwich.

Frances shifted her position. How hard it was to stay still.

A mouse darted over the floor and vanished behind the skirting boards.

Soft steps alerted her. They'd left the door unlocked. A simple push sufficed to release the catch.

The steps moved closer.

She took a deep breath. Now. She had to act now.

"Do you have my guarantee?" Did she sound like Katherine? Hopefully he'd attribute any difference in their voices to her nerves, if at all.

"Do you have my money?"

"It's close by."

He moved.

"Stay where you are," she demanded. "Put your receipt on the wooden toy lorry by the wardrobe and push it over to me."

"And if I don't?"

"Then there's no money."

"We'll see to that."

He moved fast, faster than Frances had anticipated. He jumped at the person on the sofa. His hands grasped her neck.

"What the hell?" He stared at the shop window mannequin they'd borrowed from a fashionable store. To Frances's dismay, he also stepped on the throw – and her sleeve.

She pulled herself free and rolled out from under the sofa.

He grabbed her arm.

"Stop," Sir Reginald ordered.

Frances's assailant didn't listen. Don't panic, she told herself.

He reached for her throat.

She cried out, a yell meant to distract him. Then she closed her eyes and performed exactly the movements Poppy and Dash had taught her.

With an almighty thud, Billy, employed as man at the Athena Club, crashed to the floor. Jack, who'd shared the wardrobe for the last hour with Sir Reginald, pulled Frances into his arms. It was over.

"You're under arrest for blackmail and for the murder of Walter Piggott," Sir Reginald said. He aimed a revolver at the man. "I wouldn't move if I were you. I'm an excellent shot." With his free hand, he held a police whistle to his lips and blew twice.

Billy's features distorted with fury, but he had the good sense to keep still. "It was all their fault. Cheap little tarts, leaving us to die in the trenches while they ran off with the next man."

"What about Walter Piggott? Did he deserve it too what you did to him?" Frances asked.

"I had to, didn't I? With the tart demanding to see her hubby? She'd have kept harping on, and I needed the money. I deserve the money."

"What have you done with George Blake?" Sir Reginald asked.

Billy broke into laughter. "You ain't so smart after all. It's almost worth it, seeing your faces."

"That's enough."

Two burly police officers marched in, batons and handcuffs at the ready.

Sir Reginald gave Frances and Jack a sign to sneak away.

Chapter 28

"Is it really over?" Sarah implored Frances and Katherine as they sat in her living room.

"You have nothing more to fear," Katherine said.

"It's true, I promise," Frances said. Jack had been unwilling to let her go, after her close brush with a murderer, but she'd insisted. Sarah needed to hear the truth, the sooner the better.

"We're pretty sure George did die in the war after all. It stands to reason. Nobody's ever seen him since, and as soon as you demanded a meeting, a fatal accident was arranged to make you believe you'd seen him, before he died. That allowed Billy to officially take over as a second blackmailer."

"But he knew things only George could have known," Sarah fretted.

"Men talk, especially during the war, and when you only have a few buddies. There were two men George was said to have been matey with. One was called Carl, the other William, or Billy as he was called at the Athena Club. Three men who didn't think much of women. Billy's fiancée had dumped him and married another man while he was in Flanders."

"This wound must have festered, and then seeing all the women at the Athena Club thrive, must have rankled even more," Katherine said.

"Still, I don't understand how he could have known who I was, if George is dead after all," Sarah wondered.

"Sheer good luck for him, I assume. You did talk about your first husband once, with Emily. Possibly you even mentioned the regiment, or something else pointing in the right direction."

"She wouldn't have told anyone." Sarah shrank back in her chair.

"Emily, no. But you said that you had your arm bandaged. I assume that was Dot, with maybe Billy fetching her the first aid material, or she left the door ajar," Katherine said.

"She could just as easily have mentioned it to Billy, if she was upset about it. She'd lost her sweetheart during the war, and there you were, cheering that yours didn't make it back. Billy was her stepbrother, after all," Frances said. "Anyway, it wasn't hard for him to slip into the office and go through your applications. It's all neatly filed away and as the man, he had every opportunity to search while everyone else was asleep. If he hadn't been greedy, he might have gotten away with it. You paid to keep him quiet, and if he'd kept to a smaller sum, he could have bilked you again later. Putting the screws on Emily so soon was also stupid."

"That's how we – how Frances cooked up a plan to offer him an even bigger target. All it took was a not overly private heart-to-heart with Dot, and there I was the next day, earmarked for extortion as well," Katherine said.

"What about your reputation? And as for Frances, impersonating you in a direct confrontation – that was incredibly risky." Sarah clasped their hands.

"I had a much better chance at rumbling him, because I was unexpected," Frances said. "And I couldn't have put my own mother-in-law in danger." She tactfully omitted to mention that she had enough experience as a sleuth and athletic skills honed by acting as Uncle Sal's stage assistant. As formidable as Katherine was, she lacked these things, as well as Frances's youth.

They left Sarah lost in what Frances supposed were happy dreams.

Uncle Sal dragged them inside the instant they arrived on Aunt Mildred's doorstep. "We're on tenterhooks. Jack wasn't willing to say a single peep without you." He held Frances at arm's length and gave her the once-over. "You're alright, Franny?"

"Good as gold." She pecked him on the cheek, thinking about how to phrase her story so he didn't worry in retrospect. Uncle Sal was a tough old bird, but there were occasions when he tended to fuss over her like a hen over her chicken. To hear about her wrestling, or rather jiu-jitsuing, a killer might be one of those.

Aunt Mildred welcomed her with a heart-felt hug. Katherine received a warm handshake. "I think a drink is what the doctor ordered. Tommy's rung up to say he'll be over in a tick, and we can't have him miss out on more fun."

Fun? Frances's mouth twitched. She saw Jack also crack a smile. In hindsight, it had felt good to prove their sleuthing skills. If only poor Walter Piggott hadn't paid the price.

She said as much when Tommy finally put in his appearance, together with Sir Reginald.

"Don't blame yourself," Sir Reginald said. "Piggott was long intended to be the scapegoat, if needed. It's inconceivable that Billy'd been able to secure his services at such short notice, not to mention those unspeakable garments."

"Too right. He did say that his luck had turned. I believe he'd originally been selected to deliver letters. Billy can't have intended to take care of them himself more than once or twice. The slack managing of the club helped him, but it would have been suspicious if he was spotted too often around the pigeon-holes," Jack said.

"He's admitted as much." Sir Reginald took out his cigarette case and offered it around. Only Tommy and Jack accepted a smoke. "He's gone all to pieces. His confession alone is enough to put him away, should he be spared the long drop. The police are searching his rooms as we speak."

"What about the club? Was Dot involved?" Frances had been mulling that question since they'd figured out who the blackmailer was. A portion of that money would go a long way towards restoring the old standards the members of the Athena Club were used to.

"He denies it." Sir Reginald took a deep drag. "I'm inclined to believe him."

"Poor Dot. I can't believe the board will let her stay on as manageress," Katherine said.

"We still have another problem on our hands."

"We do?" Frances was taken aback. "I thought we'd agreed there was only one blackmailer all along, and he admitted to murdering Walter."

"It's the trial." Sir Reginald finished his cigarette. "I don't see how your friend's name can be kept out of it. The connection between Billy and George set the whole scheme in motion and it was blackmailing the widow that ultimately led to the murder."

"Then we haven't helped her at all." Frances felt sick. "If the reporters get hold of her story, she'll never live it down. Who believes that she has a clean conscience if she paid for Billy's silence?"

"That's the crux. I'm sorry I haven't got better news, at least for now."

Tommy interrupted the heavy silence that followed Sir Reginald's words. "I say, Frances, I wish I'd seen you make short work of that brute."

"So do I. I wish you'd have given him a bloody nose or worse." Aunt Mildred smiled at her, the epitome of an aristocrat with her adored corgi on her lap.

Frances interpreted Tommy's wistful gaze. "If we push the table in the library aside, I'll show you."

"Jolly good." Tommy rubbed his hands.

"How exciting." Aunt Mildred studied her nephew with a fond gaze. "You're not going to hurt him, Frances?"

"I say, it's more likely I could hurt her. Not that I would, of course," Tommy protested.

Jack winked at Frances. "Be gentle with him."

"Very amusing," Tommy said.

On Aunt Mildred's insistance, the thickest Persian was placed on the library floor. The furniture blocked the doorway. The servants had already been given the afternoon off, or their mistress might have gained a reputation for hitherto well-hidden eccentricity, Frances thought. Well, at least well-hidden apart from a fast friendship with stage folk and other commoners.

"You stand here." Frances showed Tommy to his spot. "I'm rolling out from underneath the sofa, scramble to get upright, and then you pounce."

"Wait a second." Sir Reginald corrected their posture.

"You'd have made a good stage director. That eye for detail is a gift," Uncle Sal marvelled.

"There are certain job similarities." Sir Reginald chuckled.

"What next?" Tommy asked.

Sir Reginald told him.

"Just say the word if I'm grabbing too hard," Tommy said to Frances.

Then he stopped talking because he hit the floor.

"Are you hurt?" She peered at him, worried as he caught his breath.

"You caught me by surprise, that's all. Once more."

Frances obliged.

"Good lord," Katherine whispered. "To think it only took a couple of lessons to teach her that."

Tommy's jaw dropped.

"I wouldn't mind having a go myself," Aunt Mildred said.

"Not with me and not today." Tommy dusted himself off. "I must say, I'm impressed. Relieved too, considering you were left to fend off a man only too happy to kill you."

"I'd have shot him first," Sir Reginald said. "And Jack was also well prepared. What a pity you're set on returning to Australia. The three of you have a skillset most of my people will never acquire."

Chapter 29

When she arrived at the Athena Club, Katherine half expected to find it closed until further notice and guarded by a police constable. Yet the doors were open, and she spotted Dot, sitting in her office. True, the manageress appeared to be frozen, from what little Katherine observed through a two-inch-wide gap in the door. At least she hadn't been arrested. Or were the police searching for more evidence and had ordered Dot to stick around?

The new maid was nowhere to be found, but the other guests seemed unaware of what had transpired.

Katherine waved them a quick good night. She sank onto her bed. How tempting the thought was to pack her suitcase and escape home. Yet for some peculiar reason she felt duty bound to stay, if only to see for herself in the morning that the pigeon-holes were empty apart from the regular post.

Jack and Frances deserved their privacy too. She shuddered to think that she'd almost insisted on playing her role to the very end. Twenty, no, ten years ago she'd have been equal to fending off Billy. As loath as she was to admit it, she was no longer a spring chicken.

She wondered about her husband. His own club was only a few miles away, offering him more comfort than she enjoyed at the moment, and a distinct lack of lawlessness. One day she'd tell Charles everything, in a sanitised version.

First, though, she'd see what the morning would bring.

It brought with it an urgent summons. The parlour maid, gawky and flustered, had just served Katherine her breakfast and left, when she came running back. "There's a phone call, Ma'am, and it's ever so important," the girl said, breathlessly.

"I know the way. You can return to your work." Katherine smiled at the young girl who couldn't be much older than 15.

"Ta ever so much. It's a right old muddle we're in, cook says. What with the new maid having scarpered last night, without so much as a bye-yer-leave." She clapped her hand over her mouth. "Pardon me. I dunno what's come over me, to speak so freely."

"I won't breathe a word to anyone." What on earth could have happened now, she asked herself as she took a last sip of tea to fortify herself.

The office door still was ajar. Dot though, could not be glimpsed. Katherine picked up the receiver. "Hullo?"

"Can you come over at once?" Jack asked.

A chill ran over her. To have her unflappable son of all people, speaking to her in such a brusque manner, was unheard of.

"Where? Home?"

"Aunt Mildred's."

"I'll be right there."

She almost ran into the parlour maid who carried a tray towards the breakfast room. She apologised.

The maid grabbed the tray harder. "Would you like me to bring you fresh toast, Ma'am?"

Katherine's stomach reminded her that she'd buttered a slice but left it uneaten. Would another five minutes make a difference?

She ate in record time and grabbed coat and hat. Aunt Mildred's limousine waited already outside the club. The Honourable Tommy Clifton opened the door for her. "Make yourself comfortable."

"Is Jack okay? And Frances?"

"All's hotsy-totsy. Relax."

He steered the car into the traffic. Once they'd left the residential streets, it seemed to Katherine as if every single vehicle in town had conspired to block their progress. She stole a glance at Tommy's care-free demeanour. "I thought you'd be at work. Whitehall, isn't it? I've forgotten your job title."

Not that she'd ever walked the corridors of power or had an idea about the inner workings, but any kind of chitchat helped distract her.

"I'm more of a dogsbody," he admitted cheerfully.

"I don't believe that for a second, if you have Sir Reginald's trust." And Jack's, she added to herself.

"He's a frightfully good sort, isn't he? To be honest, it's not often I get to do more than just routine stuff." He observed the traffic obstacles. "Hold on."

"Why?" She'd barely finished the word when he careened around the corner, causing her to slide in her seat.

"Sorry about that. Bally lorries, but this route should be better."

It was. A few minutes later, he ushered Katherine inside the house. To her surprise, Sir Reginald again appeared next to Tommy's aunt. He must have a personal interest in the case, she decided. Otherwise, there was no reason for a man of importance like him to deeply involve himself in what was after all nothing of real importance except for the victims.

Frances offered Katherine the seat next to Jack. "Before I have a heart-attack, please tell me what on earth this all is about?" Katherine asked. Her words came out sharper than intended.

Jack patted her shoulder. "It's two things and it's your tact and common sense that's needed."

"So, not another murder hunt or other dangerous stunts?"

"Heavens, no.We're much obliged for your assistance and your courage," Sir Reginald said. "You're well acquainted with both ladies targeted by Billy's machinations."

She nodded.

"He was found dead in his cell this morning. He'd already signed a complete confession but must have decided this was the only way to spare his stepsister from being dragged into a trial which surely would have ruined her. He insisted she had no involvement at all in his schemes."

"No trial. That means Sarah and Emily's stories won't become public fodder?" Katherine relaxed. She hadn't noticed how tense she'd been these last few days.

"They're spared from any scrutiny," Sir Reginald confirmed.

"Thank heavens."

Aunt Mildred twinkled at her. "You're best suited to share the good news with them. There's one last issue for us to deal with."

Katherine was puzzled.

"The Athena Club. We'll do our best to avoid a scandal, yet it's obvious there need to be changes if Lady Pemberton's pet project is to survive," her hostess said.

"We thought you could come up with practical ideas." Jack gave his mother a grin that warmed her heart. "You've got a direct line to the inner workings and insights into what the ladies really need."

"What about Dot?" Katherine asked.

"I'll talk to the board if there's a way to keep her on. There's also the matter of one trustee starting the financial decline, which led to economising everywhere, including supervision and safety. Had there been a full-time porter or doorman, Billy might not have been able to act with such impunity."

"Lady Mildred's right. We can attempt to salvage the club's reputation and existence, but only if the necessary changes are set into motion, not to please the board but to serve the members," Sir Reginald said.

"I already have one idea, a practice room for instructions in jiu-jitsu. My nephew's willing to repeat his role he demonstrated so well with Frances." Aunt Mildred chuckled.

"I say, Aunt Mildred! Dash it all, it wouldn't be the done thing for me to go around attacking elderly —"

Tommy caught his aunt's icy glare and shrank back. "Attacking ladies."

"We'll see. Anyway, I intend to learn, and I expect you to support my endeavours."

"You've made up your mind?" The young man sounded resigned.

"Indeed, I have. Sal's also willing to pitch in."

"Where is he?" Katherine asked.

"Auditioning for another part," Tommy said. "I dropped him off at the film studio at the crack of dawn. Dashed demanding profession."

"He'll be spiffing," Frances said with utmost conviction. "It's the role of a lord whose undeserving nephew is trying to trick him into leaving his fortune to him."

"A lord! He has gone up in the world," Katherine said. "Wasn't his first part as a knife-thrower."

"He's a man of many talents," Frances praised her godfather

"He is. Now, back to business before I have to return to my official duties," Sir Reginald said.

Katherine switched her attention to him.

Frances and Jack stole out of the room.

With Tinkerbell and Leo ambling side by side, Jack and Frances headed for the square. "The first crocus!" Frances stopped to admire the clumps of flowers poking out from under the trees.

The dogs reacted to her happy exclamation with wagging tail-stubs and excited sniffing.

"Careful." Frances steered them away. "Do you have any idea if those flowers are safe for dogs?"

"Tink's smart enough to stay clear of dangers, and he's teaching Leo well. I'm much more inclined to worry about your safety."

She snuggled against him. "Not with you and Uncle Sal by my side." She spotted a squirrel. "I'll miss all this, but I'm also counting the days until we're home. Is that crazy?"

"Not at all. It's been good-oh to see my mother and a new way of life, but enough's enough."

"Do you suppose Uncle Sal will agree to return to Adelaide?" She knitted her brows. "He's so happy to have landed work in the pictures, and he and Aunt Mildred are such good friends. I'd hate for him to give this up, yet I can't imagine life without him."

"We'll find out soon enough. As long as he's content, that's all that matters. And that you don't regret having married me and enduring London at its greyest and most inviting."

"London is heaven, and so was Paris. But home, that's you, and Adelaide."

"I'll drink to that, tonight at the Savoy Grill."

Her mouth flew open. "Isn't that frightfully posh?"

"You deserve it. Before you ask, it's going to be just the two of us. No Uncle Sal, no mother, no members of the British aristocracy. Only Mr. and Mrs. Jack Sullivan, stepping out for a night on the town. If you'd like a new dress for the occasion, we can take care of that too."

"I'd like that very much, as long as the prices are not daylight robbery." She chuckled.

He broke into the special grin he reserved only for her. "No daylight robbery for us or any other kind of crime. We've had more than our fair share already."

"Too right. A nice quiet life sounds bonzer right now."

He quirked his eyebrow at her.

"Well, not too quiet," she admitted. "But just us, the Top Note, and all our friends. I can definitely do without murder investigations."

Tink pressed his front paws against her legs and woofed. "He agrees, too." She tucked her arm into the crook of Jack's elbow. "I can't believe we're really alone. Let's make the most of it while it lasts."

"In that case, how about a visit to a picture palace after dinner? There's a new mystery, The Chinese Puzzle."

"I'd rather watch something funny. No more crime for us."

He pulled her close. "Fingers crossed."

Acknowledge

I've long wanted to write a book set in a club for women. I hope I did it justice. If I got it even remotely right, it's thanks to the generous support from the University Women's Club and especially Alex Maitland, the last manager of the the New Cavendish Club wich closed in 2014. The NCC was founded in 1914 by Lady Margaret Ampthill as the Voluntary Aid Detachment Club and it served as inspiration for my Athena Club.

Any errors are entirely my own.

My greatest thanks as always go to Fiona Leitch, writer, editor, note-giver, and friend extra-ordinaire, as well as to all the readers who've taken Jack and Frances (and Uncle Sal, of course) to their hearts from day one.

About the author

Carmen has spent most of her life with ink on her fingers, cozy crime plots on her mind (thank you, Agatha Christie) and a dangerously high pile of books and newspapers by her side.

She has worked as a newspaper reporter on two continents and always dreamt of becoming a novelist and screenwriter.

When she found herself crouched under her dining table, typing away on a novel between two earthquakes in Christchurch, New Zealand, she realised she was hooked for life.

The shaken but stirring novel made it to the longlist of the Mslexia competition, and her next book and first mystery, The Case Of The Missing Bride, was a finalist in the Malice Domestic competition in a year without a winner. Since then she has penned several more cozy mysteries, including the Jack and Frances series set in the early 1930s.

In real life, Carmen is absolutely law-abiding, has never met a ghost or been able to communicate with pets (sad, but true). The only time she shed blood and swatted a fly was by accident.

Her wanderlust has led her to live in Germany, New Zealand, and the UK. She currently lives in Italy with her human and her four-legged family.

If you want to keep in touch with her and find out more about her work, writing life, and other related things, sign up for her newsletter on her website www.carmenradtke.com and receive a free quick read!

Also by Carmen Radtke

The Jack and Frances cozy 1930s mysteries
A Matter of Love and Death
Murder at the Races
Murder Makes Waves
Death Under Palm Trees
The Mystery of the Christmas Bauble (a novelette)
The Case of the Christmas Angel (a novella)

The Genie and Adriana Darling cozy paranormal mysteries
Genie and the Ghost
Ghost Takes A Vacation
Ghost Stirs The Pot
Ghost and the Haunted House
Ghost Conquers the Castle

The Alyssa Chalmers Victorian mysteries
The Case of the Missing Bride
The Prospect of Death
The Tunnels of Doom (coming in 2025)

The cozy contemporary Eve Holdsworth mysteries

Let Sleeping Murder Lie
Murder on the Airwaves
A Dash of Deceit
Death at the Dog Show

Stand-alone novels
Dig Your Own Grave
Walking in the Shadow

Printed in Great Britain
by Amazon

57764330R00098